I0619741

Killa Season

Sa'id Salaam

Published by Black Ink Publications, 2020.

KILLA SEASON

First edition. April 13, 2020.

Written by Sa'id Salaam.

Prologue

"He's not really so tough you know? I probably could have taken him myself. I saved his life you know?" Doc assured his frustrated date for the night.

"Mm hm, si papi." Rosalinda smiled politely even though she inwardly wished he would shut the fuck up and get back to the task at hand.

"Who talks while eating pussy?" She wondered as she gently guided his face back into her eager crotch. He was an excellent vagina eater but kept stopping to talk. He would lick her right to the outskirts of Orgasmville then start talking again.

"Besides, he uses guns and bombs. Me, I've killed with my bare hands; squeezed the miserable life right out of that miserable bitch!" Doc announced growing hard at the memory.

Rosalinda had no clue of what the gringo doctor was talking about. All that mattered was he was an American and a chance at a better life. She planned on fucking a green card or visa or something out of the man. Giving up on the half ass attempt at oral sex and pulled him up. She used two fingers to guide his four inches inside of her. That shut him up. Pussy has a way of making one lose his train of thought so Doc became silent and stroked. Her soft moans combined with his grunts and the squishing of her wetness in a beautiful medley: A sexual symphony.

"You like that?" Doc asked needlessly as a strong orgasm overwhelmed the young woman. She frowned slightly thinking he might start talking again. Once her convulsions subsided, he guided her over on her flat stomach.

Rosalinda complied and put an arch in her back that tilted her ass in perfect position for back shots. Doc eased back into her wetness and swam for shore. He was almost there when he reached over and pulled

1

the cord from his pants pocket. She was almost there when he slipped it around her neck.

The combination of sensations had the doctor on the verge of a climatic explosion. The vagina of Latin women is a full eight degrees warmer than any other race, hence the term 'good, hot Spanish pussy.' The heat from the box combined wit her thrashing around from being strangled pushed Doc over the hedge. Oh, the irony.

Rosalinda quickly realized that this was more than sick yankee perversion. All of the white men she had sex with always wanted more than regular sex. She peed on quite a few and a couple paid their way into her other holes. No, this was more than that, he was killing her. The woman kicked, clawed and squirmed while screaming a terrible scream that never made it past her thoughts. She could feel her life seeping away with every second that passed. Then she passed. Feeling the sudden limpness of death got the doctor off with a loud grunt.

"See! I'm the real killer! Me!" He huffed into a muted ear. He childed the corpse for a few minutes while he was still deep inside of it. Well not deep, since he only had a four inch dick, but he was still in her.

Once the shivers of his climax ceased, Doc extracted himself from the vagina before it got cold. He sat upon his bed and basked in post mortem bliss before getting dressed.

"What a pretty set of lips." Doc gushed as he used a surgical scalpel to remove them from between her legs.

Doc dragged the body through his modest villa out the back of the house. The fruit tree littered yard ended at a precipice high over the beautiful country side. He took a few moments to savor the warm night. He couldn't help but to appreciate the bright lights of nearby San Jose. Even as he tossed Rosalinda's now empty shell off the cliff.

It was too dark to watch the body drop down the hillside, so he had to settle for the sound of her body bouncing down the ragged cliff. It landed with a satisfying thud along side of the others.

Yes, others! Doc had been a very naughty boy since fleeing to Costa Rica. Maybe it was the monotony of the village or maybe his former patient had rubbed off on him. Whatever it was, he was becoming quite a Killa.

Chapter 1

"You ok?" Killa asked proudly as he watched Kitty walk on wobbly legs to the bathroom. He gave himself a mental pat on the back for a job well done.

"Ha ha, very funny!" Kitty quipped. "Boy, I swear you greedy. I said you could have some pussy but you all in my stomach. Just hard-headed."

"They don't call me Killa for nothing." He laughed.

Kitty stuck her tongue out at him before entering the bathroom. Once inside she lathered a plush washcloth in warm suds to wash the sexual secretions from her and her man.

Killa leaned back in the satisfaction a man feels when he knows he just beat the pussy up. The comfort that comes from when your woman is sexually fulfilled. He knew he put on too. Hit it so well he wished he had a commentator, like from a horse race or something, or maybe judges with score cards. He was one of the smart men who knows not to leave his woman sexually frustrated. That's why mailmen and cable guys get so much pussy. They stumble across sex starved women all day. Not Killa's woman though. He gave her the business.

If he was a cigarette smoker he would have smoked one just then. He wasn't so he lit the half a blunt that served as mental foreplay before the physical. Again he was one of the smart men who made love to a woman's entire being. Extended foreplay to ensure every need was met. Kitty came out and began washing his genitals as he exhaled his first drag.

"Boy, stop." Kitty laughed as she felt him begin to stiffen again in her hands.

"What can I say, you'se a sexy mother fu..." The sound of one of Killa's phone stopped him in mid-sentence and propelled him from the bed. Like most professional people, the hired gun had several phones for business but this one was personal.

"Grandma, you ok?" He asked urgently upon answering the call on the rarely used satellite phone.

"No, I am not alright! Thisnastyasslittleboydonebrokeintomyhouse,stoleallmystuff, beatmygranddaughterup.!" She blurted out in one run-on sentence.

"Grandma, I have no idea what you just said." He said trying to stifle a laugh. He hadn't heard her upset since he was a little boy and she figured out that he was the one killing all the junkies in the projects. She told him, "Boyyoubetterstopshootingallthedamncrackheadsbeforethedealersgetonyourbuttformessinguptheirmoney,gotthepolicedownhereeverydaypickingup...."

"I said! This nasty little boy, Ms. Jean's grandson, broke into our apartment and cleaned us out! He stole all my jewelry and Cameisha's college money. Then, the little....nigga. Yes, I said nigga! He beat my baby up! Poor thing walking around with knots on her head." Grandma huffed.

The sweet old lady was seething at the invasion of privacy and the harm to her family. Having a stranger in your home, your bedroom, rummaging around picking through your personal belongings is just a level below rape. She felt totally violated at the thought. The little bastard had even left her only pair of thongs on the floor. That was bad but what happened to her grandchild was worse. The police could have handled the theft but the beating called for death so she called for a killer. "I want you to come and talk to them all!"

"I'll see you tonight, love you." Killa said and clicked off.

"Where are you going babe?" Kitty asked still caressing his semierect manhood. It had been cleaned but she didn't want to let it go.

"Man, I gotta go home and talk to the kids in my projects." He replied, making it sound like he was a guest motivational speaker at a youth group.

Grandma knew he didn't do any talking. Call a counselor or politician if you want a speech. Call Killa and he's coming to murder everything moving.

"I guess I'd better get me one for the road then." Kitty purred; then replaced the warm wash cloth with her hot mouth.

After sucking him fully erect, she climbed on board. Just before mounting, she changed her mind and turned around to ride him backwards. Killa picked up the smoldering blunt as she slid down the length of his pole. She treated him to the triple treat of the sight, sounds and feel as she worked her ass and hips in harmony.

Since Kitty had everything under control, the killer took pulls on his weed and enjoyed the show. The couple had become sexually synced and totally in-tune with each other. A half an hour after climbing on top of him, Kitty rode them to a mutual climax.

"You probably scared all the birds out of the trees with that scream when you came." Killa laughed once he caught his breath.

"Um babe, that was you!" Kitty shot back. Truthfully.

Chapter 2

Killa was on high alert as he strolled through Atlanta's Hartsfield Airport. A fitted cap pulled low along with the throngs of people provided a moving mask to conceal his identity. The precaution was futile as dozens of security cameras randomly ran faces through facial recognition software to compare against wanted criminals and known terrorists. Killa was both but the facelift he received from the deceased doctor made him invisible.

"Round trip to Newark please." Killa responded to the flirtatious ticket agent.

"Business or pleasure?" The cute Asian woman asked as she flashed an even cuter smile. She leaned forward to allow a peak at her breasts in her partially buttoned blouse.

"Oh pleasure." Killa gushed accepting the free peek. He enjoyed killing in general but to murder someone who violated his family made his dick hard or was it the pretty young thing in front of him. "I don't mean to be crass but I would love to fuck your brains out when I get back."

"That would be my pleasure." She smiled sliding her number along with his tickets.

Killa and Kitty had an open relationship but Kitty never acted on it. She was content with being his number one. His home was in her heart and she knew it. When he was in town, he was with her. There were no mistresses or booty calls. There was no one special.

"What about Sincerity?" Killa heard himself ask. "What about her?" He shot back curtly.

Sincerity was the younger sister of his one time best friend Rico. Killing Rico never bothered his conscience the least. Dude deserved it, asked for it and got it. Killa put him on, allowing him to put food in the fridge; and he stole. You do dirt, you get dirty. Rico's death forced his mother off drugs and created a better environment for young Sincerity. He always kept an eye on the pretty young girl until she grew into a pretty woman.

Speculation ran rampart when the project diva named her only son Xavier. She never even told the boy's father he had a child. In reality, Killa and Sincerity had never acted on their mutual attraction. She was too young back then and he was too busy now. She was; however, the only one he trusted to keep an eye on his people.

After finally making it through the security procedures, he made his way to the terminal. Luckily for him, he didn't have a Muslim name like Sa'id Salaam or a big beard like Sa'id Salaam, so they didn't pull him out of the line for extra search like they do Sa'id Salaam.

With an hour to wait, he strolled into a bookstore in search of distraction. He found the African-American section tucked in a back corner of the store. The rows were cramped with similar titles and covers but one caught his eye.

"SEX AND VIOLENCE, huh?" Killa laughed as he plucked the latest novel from Amira QueenPen from the crowded shelf. "Sounds right up my alley!"

The book busied his brain from Georgia to Jersey and before he knew it, they were landing in Newark. By the time he finished, he was ready for part two like everyone else.

Killa traveled light, only carrying a carry-on bag. It contained two changes of clothes and nothing more. One for murder and the other for the return trip. He got a kick out of the middle-aged white lady in the window seat starring at his dick print when he put the bag in the overhead bin. Thoughts of Kitty gave her a better show when he pulled it down upon arrival. He took a deep breath, inhaling the cool summer night air when he stepped outside.

"Taxi?" A foreign cabbie inquired with a deep accent from wherever he was from. For reply, Killa opened the back door and climbed in.

"How much to go across the bridge? To the Bronx?"

"Four hundred!" The greedy driver lied. He was gonna send half of that home to his wife and family in his country and buy some pussy with the rest.

"A-yo, do I look like a tourist or some shit? Do I fucking sound like I'm from Europe? Huh!" Killa shot back enraged at the extortion attempt. In his youth, he would have agreed to the price, paid it, and then put a bullet in his head once they got there.

"Sorry, sorry, one hundred." The driver corrected upon hearing murder in his tone. The threat of death is a powerful negotiation tool.

"That's more like it." Killa said calming down. He leaned back into the backseat for the ride across the bridge.

Crossing the George Washington Bridge into New York at night is just shy of spectacular. The only thing that tops it is flying into the city at night. Killa's mind slipped into murder mode once they crossed the next bridge into the Bronx.

"Pull over here." Killa ordered once they reached 170th street.

"Here?" The driver asked fearfully at the request. There was nothing on the darkened corner but death.

"Yeah, here!" Killa barked and thrust a hundred dollar bill forward. The driver exhaled a sigh of relief at the sight of the money. He survived tonight but it was only a matter of time until he was found slumped behind the wheel of his cab.

Killa got out and gave his Yankees cap a tug down to conceal his face, as he took the back streets to the projects. No one paid the stranger much attention as he strolled quickly through the projects except, a group of Five Percenters looking for a lick. They beamed in on him when he pulled out his smart phone and tapped out a quick text.

The text went to the occupant of his first destination. It ensured that the resident was ready for his arrival. He rushed up to the third floor and the door was opened as he walked down the hall.

"Damn!" was all that came to mind at the sight of Sincerity holding the door open.

The tiny pink shorts she had on were pulled up snugly into her crotch displaying a fat camel toe. Not one of those fake camel toes that are mostly hair, as she was shaved bald. No, this was all rabbit. The matching half shirt was held up royally by a heavy pair of breasts with nipples poking through. A faint brown line ran down the faint pouch of her stomach; a treasure trail leading to a pot of honey. Killa liked honey. He felt light-headed as a rush of blood ran from one head to the other.

"Stop playing." Sincerity giggled as if she hadn't gotten the reaction she was going for. She knew that 'lil sister' pat on the head shit was out. He looked at her like a man looks at a woman.

"I didn't expect you so early or I would have put some clothes on." She lied. She put those clothes on for him.

Killa shot a curious glance at his watch as he entered and saw it was exactly the time he told her he would arrive. She leaned in for a hug and he took it but only half-way. He didn't want her to feel the instant erection she gave him.

"This is nice." Killa nodded once they broke off the lopsided hug. He looked around the decked out project unit with approval. The floors were layered in thick carpet and walls covered in mirrors. The leather furniture had no idea it would be stuffed inside of a tiny project apartment but it made itself at home. A huge flat screen dominated one of the small walls.

Likewise, the kitchen was decorated in faux brick and loaded with gadgets the diva barely used. Expensive pots and pans set lived in the cabinets along with the fine china.

"Thanks to you!" Sincerity shot back with a grateful smile. It was all paid for by the generous allowance he sent her for keeping an eye on his grandmother.

It was a little more than that though. He had been looking out for her since he killed her brother years back. He viewed her like the little sister he never had. Until now, that is, with the big her big caramel thighs.

"Did you get that from your pops?" He asked as he plopped down onto the plush leather. He sought to deflect the praise and get down to the business at hand.

"I did! Karate Joe came through A.S.A.P." She cheered in support of her eccentric father. She jumped up quickly causing everything to jiggle and rushed off to her room to retrieve his order.

Killa could only shake his head as he watched her fat ass bounce from side to side as she walked away. He couldn't help but notice how much she had filled out. The five-year age difference was tremendous and insurmountable when they were young but totally insignificant now. She could get it.

"Ta-dah!" Sincerity announced as she returned. She posed with the huge 10 millimeter pistol by her curvy hip. He couldn't take his eyes off either. Her other hand held the large screw-on silencer because bad boys move in silence and violence.

"Impressive!" He exclaimed standing to accept and inspect the handware.

"I'll say!" Sincerity gushed at the bulge in his pants.

"So, tell me about these niggas who robbed my people?" Killa asked shifting attention from his dick: Momentarily anyway.

"Well, their ring leaser is Tay, Ms. Jeans grandson. Word is he was dating your niece and lifted the keys, waited til they were out and hit'em up. Yo shorty snuffed him in front of building 1440 but his boys jumped in. Beat that girl like a grown man!" She said hotly.

"What's up with that niece of mine?" He asked curiously.

"A-yo lil mama a trip!" Sincerity laughed. "She beat up a couple chics out here; now she their leader. But yo.......there's something in her eyes......same thing I see in yours. Word is bond, if you weren't here that business would get handled by her!"

"Same thing in my eyes?" Killa asked. He hoped not because he sees dead people. He stood to leave and handle his business which was his pleasure.

"Fall back through once you're done. I have something I wanna give you" Sincerity said nervously.

"Aww, you got me a present?" Killa chuckled.

"Been had it, I just now wanna give it to you. Want you to have it."

"Aight, Imma fall through once I'm done." He said. He planted a sisterly kiss on her forehead and slipped out into the night. "Let the killing begin!"

Chapter 3

The same pass key acquired many years back when Lil J had control of the projects allowed Kill to move freely through the housing complex. He used side and back doors restricted for maintenance to gain access to the building.

Rabbit was the first to go. He was so caught up in his video game that he didn't hear death enter his door. Killa was impressed that the teen had reached last level of the game. He had never made it that far himself so he watched for a few minutes.

"Yes! Yes!" Rabbit yelled as he soared past the old recorded and completed game.

"Bravo." Killa clapped then clapped him with the cannon. The slug tore into one of his shocked eyes and out the crater in the back of his head.

Killa turned to leave to make his round then stopped in his tracks. On a whim he grabbed the controller and put his own name on the high score. KILLA

Rabbit had a head start on his friends but Dee was next to join him. Killa stumbled upon him in the stairwell getting a sloppy blow job from a junky. The slurps and moans echoed in the hallow space. He looked up from the junky and saw Killa standing there. He frowned then opened his mouth to say something but the large bullet that sped into his open mouth had blown the words all over the wall behind him. Dee fell so fast he snatched the junky's dentures out with his dick.

"See, that's that bullshit! I ain't even got paid yet!" The crack addict protested.

"I don't think he'd mind if you took what he owes you out of his pockets." Killa offered apologetically. He was dead after all and didn't need cash for that.

One by one, Killa paid visits to all those involved in harming his family. Each and everyone of them met a brutal end. The large caliber gun ensured closed caskets for all. On his way to see the guest of honor, he ran into the group of Fiver Percenters who peeped him coming in.

"Peace God." Their spokesman offered as Killa came upon them.

"Whatever." Killa huffed, eager to finish his business.

"A-yo what's today's mathematics?" Another asked, sticking his arm out to block his path. A slow murderous grin spread on his face at the violation.

"You tell me, since you god and all." Killa replied.

"The black man is the supreme Asiatic black man. See eighty-five percent of mankind is in darkness. Ten percent are in something and five percent are true and living gods. Feel me?" The third of the three explained.

"Ok, let me see if I got this straight. You guys are god? All of you?"

"True, true. Peace god." They all agreed.

Killa quickly pulled the gun and took ten percent of one of the Five Percenters face off. The next one lost his gold grill along with his life by the next shot. The last man was shaking so hard, the change in his pockets jangled lightly.

"Ok god, resurrect your friends." Killa demanded to the survivor. "Nooooo! God did not just pee his pants!"

"Peace god, peace." The pissy thug pleased desperately.

"God is one, say it!"

"Yeah, yeah, one God, one God." He repeated nodding eagerly. "Peace god."

"Piece you mean." Killa corrected and blew pieces of the thug onto the concrete.

"That was fun!" Killa giggled to himself as he set back off for his final victim of the night.

Killa used his pass key to open the front door to Tay's apartment. His grandmother was sitting in front of the TV sipping malt liquor when he slipped inside. Even with the plastic surgery, she recognized him instantly. She had, after all watched him grow up in these same projects.

"Figured you were coming." She nodded knowingly. "Told that boy a million times to cut his shit. Second room on the right."

"K, thanks." He said and headed off to complete his task.

Tay obviously intended to make his murder easy. He has smoked himself into a weed induced coma and lay mouth wide open on his bed. It wasn't open quite far enough and he lost two teeth when Killa slammed the silencer into his mouth. When it touched his tonsils, he was wide awake.

Tay moaned loudly from pain and fear. He knew in an instant who the angry man standing over him was. Growing up in High Bridge, he'd heard tales of the monster called Killa. He was urban legend status, the subject of bedtime stories.

"Eat your vegetables or Killa's coming to get you."

"You know who I am? Why am I here?" Killa growled.

"Mmm, mmm!" Tay nodded, taking the gun in his mouth up and down. "Mmmm, mmm." He repented desperately pointing towards his dresser.

"The dresser? Is that where my sweet old grandmother's stolen shit is?" Killa asked. He would be shocked if the kid hadn't already traded the valuable trinkets for chump change.

"Mmm, mmm!" Tay nodded again. He was thankful he hadn't sold the stuff yet. Now he could just give it back and get on with his life.

"Hold this!" Killa demanded.

"Hmh?" Tay frowned at the curious command.

"The gun, hold the gun." Killa ordered, lifting his trembling hand to hold the gun in his own mouth. "And if you take it out, I'm going to shove it up your ass!"

Tay held the gun firmly in place to both of their relief. He did not want it in his ass anymore than Killa wanted to put it there. He would have to though because he was a man of his word. If there's anything worse than having a pistol shoved down your throat, it would have to be having it shoved up your ass. Talk about heads or tails.

Instead of calming the killer, the sight of his grandmother's belongings in the thug's possession only fueled his anger. He had seen these pieces on her person. The thought of him selling her jewels for blunt money infuriated him even more.

"Is this what you did with my niece's money?" He asked holding up the gaudy chain and medallion. As funny as Tay holding the gun in his mouth while nodding was, Killa didn't laugh. "Aight yo, your friends are waiting on you."

Tay breathed a sigh of relief because he didn't know his friends were all already dead. They were at the gates of hell holding the door open for him. Killa came back over and took control of the gun. Instead of pulling it out he pulled the trigger, repeatedly.

The wall behind the teen was painted an interesting pattern of red and pink from the blood, bone and brain matter; an eclectic display of modern art that probably could've fetched a pretty penny in a gallery. Killa gathered up his grandmother's stuff along with the chain and weed purchased with the stolen money.

"All done?" Ms. Jean asked when Killa re-appeared in the front room.

"All done." He replied stoically as he studied her for the need to kill her too. He found none.

"Ok, tell Ms. Deidra I'm sorry 'bout all the mess." She offered sincerely.

"I'm sorry about the mess too."

****

The project pass key didn't work at Grandma's house but no worries because he was expected. A coded knock alerted Deidre that her beloved grandson was here. She smiled brightly as she rushed to open the door.

"Let me see you!" She gushed, taking his altered face in her small hands. "how are you baby?"

"Fine, how are you?" Killa asked, getting a well needed hug. No place is more comforting than a motherly hug. It's the safest place on the planet.

"I'm fine, better now that you're here. Are you just now getting here?" She asked.

"Nah, been here for a couple of hours. Had to make my rounds." Killa replied, putting her jewels in her hand.

"My ice!" Deidra cheered and began to inspect her pieces. "What about Cameisha's money?"

"Got that too." He replied referring to the weed he confiscated. From everything Sincerity had told him about the girl, she would know what to do with it. It was as good as cash in the right hands, and she had the right hands.

Killa was able to spend a few weeks with his notorious cousin, the original Dope Boy: Cameron Forrest. The two had bonded like brothers in their brief time together. Even when Cam had to disappear on the run, he was only a phone call away.

"I'll put her stuff in her room." Killa offered and went to his old room.

"Look at you lil mama." Killa chuckled, looking down on the sleeping girl. Her beauty made him smile despite the knots and lumps on her head. She looked far better than those who gave them to her.

Killa turned to return her belongings, putting weed and chain on the dresser. A curious noise that sounded like a tiny trumpet caught his ear. He wondered what it was until the smell caught up to it.

"Ugh, you rotten." Killa laughed and fled from the funk-filled room.

"Isn't she just adorable?" Deidre gushed about her beloved grand-daughter.

"She is. You cooked cabbage tonight huh?" Killa replied.

"Yes! How'd you know? Would you like a plate?"

"The girl told me, and no. I gotta push on." He replied with a lonely sigh. It was time to disappear back into the shadow he lived under.

"So soon?" his grandmother moaned so sadly he thought about kicking the girl out his room and moving home.

"Yeah, I gotta stop by and see Sincerity before I go."

"I see." Deidra nodded knowingly. "I assume you're the reason she is always watching and speaking to me. At first, I thought she wanted beef but she cool. Cameisha thinks the world of her."

"Yeah, she's good people. I asked her to keep an eye on you girls. I trust her." Killa said emphatically. In an instant grandma trusted her too. She still had to talk some shit though.

"Grandma can take care of herself!" She huffed indignantly. "Oh and that girl in there! Please!"

****

"Man, I hope this girl aint got them tiny ass shorts on." Killa griped in a classic 'Be careful what you wish for' scenario.

People often wish for things and its not quite what they want; like asking for rain and it rains for forty days and nights, or wishing for a man and he ends up being some bullshit, or wishing for a book deal and it's not what you thought it would be.

Again, a text message announced his approach and the sound of locks turning, greeting him as he made his way down the hallway. Killa got his wish and Sincerity didn't have the little shorts on. She didn't have on anything. She stood there for a second so her nakedness could register before turning away.

"Lock it behind you." She said as she walked back to her room.

Killa let out a sigh as he watched her full ass cheeks bounce away. He knew then that the cat and mouse game was over. He followed directions and locked the locks, then followed the direction she went in. Since he shed his own clothing on the way, he too was naked by the time he reached the room.

Killa and Sincerity looked each other over silently and were both impressed. She was clean, firm and fine. He was chiseled, handsome and would be hung if not pointing his erection in her direction.

The first kiss was tentative, cautious even, soft pecks that grew in intensity until it was almost violent. Sincerity bit his lip so hard she drew blood. She reached down and practically shoved him inside of her. Abstinence left her so tight that it hurt them both.

Killa knew the bites and claws she was giving were designed to make him fuck her harder so he did. He plowed into her causing her to scream with every stroke. The sound of skin slapping together rang throughout the otherwise quiet room.

Sincerity now bit her own lip too, trying to stave off an imminent orgasm. Fighting it only increased its immensity. A deep guttural cry sounded when she finally exploded. Killa was right behind her. Her convulsions pushed him over the edge as well and he let go.

"Now what?" Killa asked once he caught his breath.

"That's on you, same as always." Sincerity replied, still squeezing him with her vagina muscles. "I'm here for you. I'm not going nowhere. Ever!"

"But why?" Killa pondered. "Ma you a bad chic, you can have any man you want."

"Remember you said that. I already been around the block so I know what's out there. I've had the so-called ballers, even a pro-ball player but that shit ain't real. Then dudes sported me like an accessory to make themselves look good, like I'm a fucking piece of jewelery or rims for their cars." Sincerity lamented sincerely.

"What about your baby daddy?" Killa asked, exploring all the options.

"That sorry ass nigga don't even know he got a kid! Well, by me at least. I tried him up and told him I might be pregnant when I found out I was. Dude mumbled something and hung up. An hour later, one of his flunkies came by with five racks for an abortion." She spat with the sting still audible in her voice.

"I gotta bounce." Killa announced. Sure it was a cop out but it was easier than dealing with emotions. Fuck emotions, feelings and sentiment. They were more trouble than good.

"Yeah, ok, gotta bounce. I'll be right here waiting. Just remember, I know you. I'm from these same grimy ass projects. No one on earth can hold you down like I can. Bet you won't look at that chic the same when you get back home!" Sincerity laughed.

She knew she just planted a seed in his mind. she also knew seeds take time to grow, so she was patient. Irony was; Killa just planted a seed too.

Thoughts of Kitty flooded the murderer's mind as soon as he stepped from the building. Visions of her smile, eyes and Kitty raced through his brain. He used the back streets to avoid prying eyes. The next time he looked up, he was at Yankee Stadium. He stuck his arm out and hailed a taxi.

"Newark Airport." Killa ordered and settled back into the seat for the ride.

"Bout a hundred bucks." The Arab cabbie announced into his eyes via the rearview mirror. Honesty lives in the iris of men, so the driver put the car in motion.

"A-yo, how far is Patterson from the airport?" Killa asked as they crossed the bridge back over to Jersey.

"Not too far. You wanna go there instead?" The driver asked.

"Think I'll have time to swing by and kill Nae before my flight? Since she thinks I got soft."

"Probably not." The cabbie shot back wide-eyed.

"Guess I'll let it slide this time. Besides, she is kinda cute."

Chapter 4

It was a rare occasion to see Killa out in public with a smile. Today was one of those rare occasions. He sat on a park bench watching children from a nearby daycare center at play. All the children brought him joy but especially the handsome little brown boy who had his mother's smile but Killa's eyes.

As much as he wanted to scoop him up and twirl him around, he knew he couldn't. Protecting his only child meant not being a part of his life; not now anyway.

"Excuse me sir, can I help you?" A frail but feisty white lady asked. The smile on her fifty-something year old face didn't mask her aggression.

"No ma'am. Just watching the children play. I'm harmless." Killa assured her. A flash of recognitions washed over her face as he spoke. Now her smile was genuine.

"Xavier is a very bright child!" She beamed knowingly. "Loving and happy except....he can be dark. The boy has a dark side."

"It runs in the family." Killa said, taking to his feet. He cast one last glance over his child and moved on.

Every time Killa got a chance to be anywhere near Pennsylvania, he made it his business to put eyes on his child. A college fund was bursting at the seams, waiting for the boy. It was one of life's pleasures but he was here on business.

****

"Forgive me father for I have sinned." Killa confessed, fighting the urge to laugh at the understatement. He never quite understood confessing to a man when God sees all that you do.

"Confess your sins my son." The perfidious pastor said convincingly. Truth be told, he could give a fuck about the next man's problems.

Confessions were a part of the job but he hated it. The shit was boring. 'I cheated on my wife. I sucked the mailman's dick. I cheated on my taxes.' Bullshit! He sometimes wanted to shout some of this own sins back through the partition and show them what a sin is.

"Can I get in trouble for what I say? I mean it's not....legal." Killa stammered, impressed with his acting. Perhaps Hollywood was calling. Can you picture Killa on the big screen!

Instead of screaming, 'Get on with it already!' The pastor bit his tongue and gently explained that conversations with clergy were privileged. "Just you and I son." He assured him. Killa took note that he didn't mention God but then again would he even be there if the pastor believed in God? Killa took a deep breath and began to recite his rehearsed script. Hollywood here we come.

"Father, I have a ...... well a fetish for boys, young ones." He began. He could actually hear the bored pastor bolt up in his seat through the partition.

"Please, go on! Spare no details!" He pleaded. The lust in his voice disgusted Killa. Luckily, he couldn't see the man pull his erection out or Killa would have said, fuck the plan and killed him right there on the spot. " Do you, do you touch them?"

"I devour them. I can't get enough. I've tried to stop but I can't. I just purchased a new one, a six year old, but I haven't opened him yet. Instead, I came here."

"A brand new six year old!" The pastor practically screamed. "His seal is still intact?"

Killa had no idea exactly what that meant but replied affirmatively, since it seemed to be a big deal to him. As soon as he said yes, he heard the man grunt from a climax. Again, Killa wanted to shoot him but knew what awaited would be so much more fun.

"What shall I do with him? I took him to my cabin because I'm not sure." Killa sighed, earning his first Oscar.

"Take me to him!" The pastor demanded urgently.

"It's a long drive from here." Killa said into the partition.

Let's go!" The pastor urged almost getting shot when he pulled opened the confessional door.

Both men spent the two hour drive in the solitude of their own minds. Killa was amazed by the scenic view of the Pennsylvania Mountains. It was yet another confirmation of God's existence. Who else could make something so mighty and majestic besides the Most Mighty and Majestic?

He planned to bring Kitty back here the first chance he got. Things had changed between them ever so subtly when he returned from New York. Kitty still had his heart and body but Sincerity ruled his thoughts.

"No one on earth can hold you down like I can."

Father Julious Miles had only one thing on his twisted mind; a brand new boy in pristine condition. In his sick circle of pedophiles, an unopened child was highly coveted. You could find some good used ones with low miles, but a new one!

"Here we go." Killa announced, pulling the pastor from his disgusting thoughts. He pulled off the main road onto a tree-lined dirt road. The road was actually a driveway that ended in front of a custom cabin.

"What's that smell?" Father Julious asked, wrinkling his nose to emphasize his aversion to the aroma.

"Hogs. We keep them out back. They help dispose of the trash." Killa replied, leading the way to the cabin. He walked up the steps with the pervert right on his heels, eager to get at the boy.

Killa unlocked the door and stepped aside to allow the pastor to enter. He closed the door behind them and locked it, tight. Father Julious scanned the dim room for his prize.

"Where is he?" He asked, desperately. "Did he leave?"

"Have a seat!" Killa demanded, pointing to the only chair in the room. It faced the only other object in the room, a large flat screen monitor mounted on the wall.

Killa hit the button on the remote and the TV filled with the face of a cute blue-eyed, blond boy.

"Yes, oh yes!" The pastor moaned lustfully. A second later a frown of familiarity contorted his face. It was that 'where do I know you from' frown.

The hired assassin hit play on the remote and the face on the screen began to age progress forty years. Its owner smiled at what must be going on in his mind right now.

"That's right! It's me; Allen, you remember me don't you?" The former victim and current client asked with a smile.

"What's going on here?" The pastor demanded, attempting to stand. The gun pointed at his face requested he stay seated. Killa paused the video to explain.

"The word in Arabic is Jazaa'ah. It can be used for good or bad, depending on what you've earned; reward or punishment, good or bad: Bad in this case." Killa relayed and restarted the recording.

"Bless me father for you have sinned." The customer began. He started off slow and calm, growing enraged as he went along. "You betrayed me; seduced me. You molested me and fucked me! You made me suck your dick, you sick fuck! Have you any idea how badly that shit fucked me up?! Do you care? I grew up not knowing if I was gay or straight. I spent years and years in therapy. I lost my wife, my family! I was told I should forgive. Let go and let God, they said. But fuck that, I want revenge. Now you pay!"

"I tried to help you! I showed you love, just like I've loved hundreds of boys like you!" The father pleaded. In his sick mind he actually believed it.

"A-yo, you do now that's a recording don't you?" Killa laughed.

"So what happens now?" He asked still confused about why he was there.

"Now you die." Killa replied nonchalantly. "I'm going to kill you. Torture and kill actually."

"Thou shall not kill!" The pastor demanded, jumping to his feet. Killa slapped him in his mouth with the broad side of his gun sitting him back in his chair.

"Thou shall not kill but butt fucking little boys is cool." Killa growled. This was business but it just turned personal.

Killa kicked and stomped on the pervert until he remembered his instructions.

"You know some of the shit on this list, I wasn't gonna do. It's going a bit far, even for me, but fuck it. I'll get over it, you won't."

The sniveling coward put up some resistance as Killa stripped him of his clothing. He dragged the naked man into the kitchen where a morticians table awaited. Killa hosted him up and strapped him down. He opened the satchel of supplies and donned a pair of rubber gloves and got to work.

"Oh God, no! Please!" The pastor pleaded when a yard long wooden dildo came into view.

"Bet them little boys said the same thing when they saw your wood." Killa retorted, taking position over the man.

In one hand was the dick shaped stake and rubber mallet in the other. Killa lined up the tip with his rectum and swung the hammer.

"Yeeeeooooowww!" The pastor screamed, shrilly from the pain.

"Yeah, I bet." Killa laughed. "Dude you missed your true calling. You shoulda been an opera singer." The preacher yelped with each pound from the hammer, pushing it deeper into his body.

"You're killing me." He said pitifully.

"Uh..yeah! Duh." Killa chided. He stopped impaling the man because he didn't actually want him to die; not just yet anyway.

"Shit!" Killa grimaced at what was next on the list. He shrugged like 'oh well' and removed a pair of wire snippers from the bag. "You took a piece of your victims every time you touched them." Killa said, explaining the next phase. Jazaa'ah indeed.

Father Julious didn't even complain when Killa began removing his fingers one at a time. The huge stake in his ass even over shadowed his toes being cut off. Next came his lips, nose and ears.

"Not doing that." Killa giggled at the next item on the list. "Good news, you get to keep your dick!"

Killa opened the back door and tossed the severed body parts out. The appetizer caused a near riot as the huge hogs fought to devour them.

"Now comes the fun part." Killa announced eagerly, as he un-strapped the man.

"You're a killer, murderer. You are going to burn in hell." The pastor wasted some of his last breath to proclaim.

"Well yeah, I may be a murderer but I never made partners with God. I can be forgiven, you should worry about your own soul. So take a few seconds to get right with God cuz in a few seconds you going to be right with God."

Killa grabbed the portion of the wood not in his ass and pulled him off the table. The hogs were in a frenzy as he drug him toward the door. The pastor begged, pleaded, and called on everyone and everything ex-cept God when he got shoved into the middle of the ravenous pigs.

"Oh shit!" Killa exclaimed in shock as they began to eat him. He giggled again and crossed off the last item off the list when one of the hogs bit his genitals off. He watched for a while until on of the animals ran off into a corner with the man's head.

"Well, that was fun." He laughed as he turned away.

Ever the professional, Killa methodically removed all traces that he was ever there. Once he was back in his car, he called to report in. The task he hated most of all.

"It's done." He announced when the call was answered.

It always irked him not to have a face to go with the voice. What was worse was the sarcastic undertones the man laced his speech with.

"As directed?" The voice replied, intently.

"Of course. I'm a professional." Killa snapped curtly.

"Very good. I just sent thrity seven five to your account."

"Thirty-seven five? Why the short" He asked of the twenty-five percent reduction in his pay.

"I decided to fine you for that unauthorized business in New York." The voice chided, grating the killer's nerves.

"Fine? Unauthorized? Son, you got me fucked up! I'll kill anybody.....anywhere, anytime I fucking feel like it." Killa shot back. "Just because we do business together, doesn't mean you own me. Never try to son me again."

"Ok see, that's where you're wrong. You are a part of the organization that I run. I do own you. I'm daddy and decided to cut your allowance. Next time I spank that ass." The voice stopped as its owner waited for his come back, but none came.

Killa didn't argue with dead people and the dude was as good as dead. He had made up his mind to murder him the first chance he got.

"Don't worry son." The voice resumed with a verbal pat on the head. "The next one is a double header. A cool hundred grand. You can buy that pretty girlfriend of yours something pretty."

The line went dead before Killa had a chance to respond. It was probably for the best though since he didn't have anything nice to say. Like the saying goes, 'Let those who believe in God and the last day either speak good or remain quiet.'

When Killa tossed his phone on the passenger seat, he noticed the recently deceased had left his phone. The man was so eager to get at the little boy.

"You so nosey." Killa sang, teasing himself as he went into the phones picture gallery.

The car swerved violently as the gross graphic images muled kicked him in his conscience. It was full of grown men with small boys. The pedophiles actually had a group where they shared pictures and videos of their conquest. They also occasionally shared little boys. He heard the warning and threat about his un-authorized killings but fuck that. "All yall niggas are dead!" He vowed.

Chapter 5

Doc had stepped his hunting ground up by selecting 'LA Discotecha.' It was a Costa Rica's premiere nightclub modeled after the legendary Club 52 in New York. He had decided to take murder to the next level, so it was only right to kill a better class of woman.

The local strays he killed from the surrounding villages barely raised an eyebrow. He longed for the infamy and notoriety of his former client. He now viewed Xavier Forrest as competition. He planned to surpass his numbers so he had some killing to do.

Doc scanned the room taking in a new face with every flash of the pulsating lights. The dance floor was jam-packed with sweaty young bodies moving to the thunderous music pounding from the huge speakers. She spotted him in the flash of the strobe before he saw her. The attraction was mutual albeit for different reasons and they both approached.

"Hola, coma te llama?" Doc asked offering up one of his pearly white American smiles.

"My name is Bonita." The future corpse said in perfect English. "And yours?"

"Why I'm Doctor...um, just Doc." He stammered, realizing that we've never used his name before. "Just call me Doc."

"Please to meet you Doctor Doc." The pretty raven-haired young woman laughed, showing a set of pearly whites herself. Her red lipstick made a start contrast against her white skin. She was perfect. She would be missed.

"Would you like to come to America with me?" Doc asked flashing another smile.

"Ha! What a pick-up line! I bet that works very well out in the villages but here in the city, not so much." Bonita laughed.

She was right too because in the impoverished towns and villages an offer to go to America will get you laid. Doc had been using the

American dream as bait to lure girls to this bed and then kill them. Besides a distraught family member or two, on occasion those girls went unnoticed. Bonita Flores was the daughter of the Chief of Police. Yeah, she was definitely going to be missed.

"Actually, I was referring to the Hotel America where I have a room." Doc said dangling the room key as proof.

"Why didn't you say so? I would love to go to bed with you." Bonita cheered. Her and her friends were Costa Rican socialites. They hit all the hot spots each night, leaving with foreigners or rich locals. It was almost a contest of sorts for the young sluts. Sleeping with rich and famous men earned cool points in their morally challenged club. An American doctor would be a nice notch in a well-notched belt.

The couple left the club hand-in-hand like an actual couple. They stole kisses and gropes as they walked over a few blocks to the hotel. It was mobile foreplay, like getting head while you drive. The upscale hotel was busy, well-lit, plus all the security cameras worked. If one were keeping score, this would be mistake number one: A hard, fast ball right up the pipe for strike one.

"Wasn't that the policeman's daughter?" A nosey clerk asked in rapid fire Spanish, as she multi-tasked. Her first job was as a hotel clerk but she worked part-time minding other people's business.

"Yes, with another man! Third this weekend." Her co-worker replied. "This one is an American." She added, remembering checking him in, in his real name.

This wreckless move of being spotted and identified was a looping curve ball for strike number two.

Doc reserved the room in advance so all of his supplies were already laid out and in place. He was so excited about taking his new hobby to the next level, he decided to skip the sex and get straight to the main event until Bonita dropped her flimsy dress that is.

"Oh my!" Doc exclaimed at the sight of her young body. Two heavy breasts stood proudly at attention on her chest like soldiers. The pale white mounds were topped by pretty pink nipples and her thong was the same shade of red as her lipstick.

"You like?" Bonita giggled quite pleased at the reaction. Se stepped out of the thong as Doc nodded his head like a bobble head doll.

"I like, I like very much!" Doc replied and moved on her. In one swift motion he scooped her onto the bed and put his tongue on her lips, the lower pair.

Ole Doc sucked several orgasms out of Bonita causing her two curse in two languages. The vagina was frothy and hot when he finished with it. He could see the ripples of heat waves from that hot Spanish box.

The little purple pill Doc took had his little pink dick rock hard. He shoved himself inside and speed humped to a quick nut. His erection stayed intact so he kept right on going. The little whore got more than she bargained for as the doctor fucked her raw.

"No mas! Por favor, no mas!" Bonita pleaded in Spanish as English had momentarily escaped her.

"Ok baby." Doc relented and slumped down on top of her. He began kissing her long, pretty neck. He was prepping it for surgery. "Let's take a shower."

"Ok Poppi." She agreed eagerly, even though she really wanted an ice pack for her throbbing vagina.

The super sharp knife beside the tub caught Bonita's eyes as she followed Doc into the shower. Doc adjusted the water to a comfortable temperature once they were both inside. More friendly kisses were passed back and forth as they washed each other affectionately.

"Turn around." Doc instructed and Bonita quickly obeyed. As he washed her back, he slipped a hand out the tub and grabbed the knife.

Bonita leaned her head back and closed her eyes. Almost as if offering herself for sacrifice. Doc took a deep breath and mentally looked down at the line he was about to cross. He exhaled and crossed it. Her head came off so quickly and easily, she didn't have a chance to put up any resistance. The body fell to the bottom of the tub as Doc turned to head face-to-face.

"Wow, still pretty." He marveled at the body-less head. The flat eyes were still open half way but the light of life was gone from them. Her mouth was gaped open from a scream that never materialized.

Doc thought twice about sticking his still erect penis into the mouth. He should have thought three times and maybe he wouldn't have done that nasty shit. The man fucked the dead head until he came. Then watched his semen run out of the severed neck.

After wrapping the head in plastic, he placed it in his bag. He was taking it with him. The amateur murderer wiped the room for prints which was really quite futile, especially since he left her box full of cum like a present for the crime lab. He should have put a bow on it too. Doc passed the same cameras that recorded his entrance as he made his exit.

Strike three! He was about to be called out. The novice may have been a killer but he was no Killa!

Chapter 6

"Hey baby!" Kitty practically screamed when she took Killa's call. It was the first time she had heard his voice in weeks.

Killa had been down in Mexico murdering cartel members for the last month and was missed. The black mob had sent him down to stir up shit between rival factions. He had been given the green light to kill in whatever manner he chose. He chose a hot machete to slice and dice men and women on both sides. He stirred up so much s hit that the two cartels engaged in all out war. That allowed the Black mob to fill the void.

"Hey ya self lady. Whatcha up to?" He replied just as happy to hear her voice as she was to hear his. They were as giddy as teenagers.

"Nothing, sitting here doing keagle exercises and thinking of you." Kitty purred.

"....Um...damn, I forgot what I was about to say." Killa laughed. Thinking about the way Kitty would squeeze him with her vaginal muscles made him so hard so fast he felt light headed.

"Oh guess what?! I lost twenty pounds!" She gloated triumphantly.

"What, you can't find your purse?" Killa, the comedian quipped. Most people never saw this soft, tender side of the murderer. He didn't do 'I love yous' but if he loved you, you knew it.

"Ha,ha. I do miss that tongue, but not for the jokes." Kitty lied. She loved his jokes and he had a mean vagina eating game. "I bought a new dress mister man, so you're gonna have to take me out on the town when you come home. When are you coming home?"

"I'm on my way as we speak. I was hoping for a nice quiet night at home. We can sit in front of the fire, sip a little wine? I can use a nice stiff brush and brush the naps on your neck."

"You are on a roll today, baby!" Kitty laughed. "As romantic as that sounds, I'll pass. I wanna go dancing."

"What Kitty wants Kitty gets." Killa agreed. Kitty treated him like a king so he had no problem returning the treatment. Fair exchange is no robbery.

Women could learn a lesson from Kitty. Instead of being mean and combative and making demands, be nice. Treat your man with kindness and be generous with the vagina. Either he will return the good treatment and everyone wins or he won't and expose himself as not the one. Stay with that dude and you settled for less than you're worth.

"And what Killa wants Killa gets. You want me to cum for you?" Kitty asked and began to masturbate before he could answer. Besides, she already knew the answer. It wasn't like he was going to say no. Picture that. It took Kitty just a couple of minutes to reach a screeching orgasm.

"That sounded like a good one, save some for me." Killa exclaimed just as his flight was announced. "See you tonight."

Killa had to use his carry-on bag to conceal his erection as he boarded the plane. It did the trick until he found his seat and had to stow the bad. He lifted it above his head and worked to stuff it into the crowded bin.

"Oh my!" The middle aged white lady seated by the window said of the bulge in his pants. Killa gave a couple gyrations with his hips for her benefit, and then sat next to her.

The lady bantered jovially from Alculpoco to Atlanta, hoping to sample what he showed off. Her husband was wealthy, generous and out of town, so a quick romp was in order. It was a payback as well, since his secretary was with him as well. No such luck because Killa had Kitty on his mind. Once they landed in Atlanta, Killa snatched the bag out and disappeared. He jumped in one of the taxis idling at the curb and left.

"Please don't be off that ass!" Killa wished as he neared his abode. Kitty was perfect in his eyes and he was worried about losing twenty pounds of her; especially ass.

His home was off the beaten path, so the taxi only took him to where one of his cars was parked. He was smart enough to have several vehicles at different locations around town. Each had fake but realistic ID, traveling money and of course guns. He may have never been a boy scout but he was always prepared.

Kitty saw the lights on the property ignite from the motion detectors. She knew it would only be one person so she jumped up. A few last minute adjustments later, she rushed to the entry foyer to greet her man.

"Tah-dah!" She cheered seductively posing in her new dress. She did a little twirl to give him a shot of her ass. "You like?"

"I like!" Killa announced enthusiastically. He was quite pleased but more relieved that her round mound of playground was still intact. She was noticeably slimmer but fine as all outdoors and that was plenty fine.

Kitty bounced up and down like a school girl, giddy from the praise. She rushed over and smothered his face with wet smooches. Killa dropped his bag and returned the affection. He guided her backwards into the living room until she fell on the sofa.

"Oh!" Kitty purred when her man hiked her dress above her full hips.

Killa dropped between her legs and removed her panties with his teeth. After a month of spicy Mexican food, Kitty's kitty tasted like candy and taste he did. It wasn't even a full minute before an orgasm shook the room. Killa kept right on going until she came again. He would have went for thirds if she hadn't stopped him

Kitty pulled him up and scrambled to free the erection trapped in his pants. She grabbed it and shoved it inside of her with an audible splash. She tossed her large legs onto his shoulders, giving it up completely. He took it too, tapping her cervix on every down stroke.

Killa closed his eyes in ecstasy but Sincerity's face forced them to open back up. This was Kitty's time so he didn't want to cheat her out of any of it. Every since his trip to New York he had been having mental threesomes with them every time he and Kitty made love. They weren't making love at the moment, they were fucking.

"Whose pussy is this!" He demanded. Demanded, not asked, because he already knew whose pussy it was. Men just like to hear it.

"It's Killa's!" She screamed in delight.

"And what's Killa doing to it?"

"Killing it!" Kitty replied just as she went over the edge and came again. Killa was right behind her and exploded inside of her. The couple kissed urgently as they convulsed from the mutual climax.

"Mmm. Daddy you need to go away and come back more often." Kitty moaned as she squeezed and released, squeezed and released.

"Be careful what you wish for. I may have to go out to Cali for a couple of days."

"When are you going to tell me what you really do? And no more of that hit man crazy crap!" She fussed sweetly.

"I told you. I'm a highly-trained assassin. I travel the globe and kill people. I wet 'em in Washington, murder in Memphis, kill in Kentucky, off 'em in Oregon, body 'em in Bolivia and..."

"Oh, stop it! Don't ell me then!" Kitty laughed, cutting him off. She pouted playfully. Since her bottom lip was poking out, Killa sucked and nibbled on it. That set off a round or two.

The night on the town was quickly forgotten about and they spent the night pleasing each other. They moved the session up to the bedroom and finally finished in the large custom-made tub.

"I love you so much!" Kitty sighed as they cuddled in the suds.

"No! Don't!" Killa, yelled sitting up straight in the tub. The look of pure horror on his face scared Kitty more than the actual outburst.

"What do you mean, don't love you?" She asked, bewildered. "How can I not?"

Killa had no reply. What could he say anyway? Loving me is suicide? Every woman who ever loved him died. From Fatimah to Denise, Renee, his mother; all dead. He was truly a hard dude to love.

Chapter 7

The Baron was a big Green Mile looking mother fucker. His huge six-foot inch frame was littered with muscles on top of muscles. The expensive Italian suite he wore bulged from pecs, quads and abs. His shiny bald head made him resemble a bowling ball because they didn't smile either. The fierce looking man maintained a menacing smile at all times.

The lieutenants all sat around the huge boardroom table wondering what this unscheduled meeting was about. Since there is no honor amongst thieves, they all were guilty of something. These were men who controlled the crews that controlled the streets for the Black Mob. Stealthy glances were stolen at the large Boss sitting silently at the head of the table. To make matters worse, they often had to endure abuse from Casper. Each of the men was killers and could easily eat the white man but it would certainly be a last meal.

"Big Rock!" Casper announced calling the meeting to order as he approached the man who went by the moniker. His voice was dripping with disdain as he read from his notepad.

Big Rock was a big dude who ran the Black mob's operations in Baltimore. He was a feared killer in his own right and wanted to slap the little white man's little white head off of his shoulders for using that tone of voice. But, knowing Casper was the man next to The Man, he swallowed his pride in a loud gulp and meekly replied, "Yes?"

"The Baron would like to know if you are smoking big rocks. Based on your recent numbers, you certainly aren't selling them." Casper chided.

"Boss we..." Big Rock began towards the large silent man until a loud slap from Casper shut him up.

All the killers in the room winced and grimaced at the disrespect. Big Rock was so mad and frustrated at not being able to strike back a tear escaped his eye.

"You don't have the right to speak to him!" Casper screamed at the top of his lungs as the sound of the slap still reverberated around the room.

"We are still having problems with that crew from New York. They have a better product at a better price." Big Rock managed through his rage.

"You can't kill a few out-of-towners in your own city?" Casper demanded, rearing back as if he were about to strike again. He wasn't actually going to hit him again. He just wanted to make him flinch knowing it would be humiliating.

"They either kill or turn everybody I sent at them." Big Rock admitted.

Casper shot a glance over to the still motion and speechless Baron before speaking.

"Guess its time to send a pro."

Casper turned his attention to the rest of the men in attendance. A few accolades but mostly ass chewing. As he spoke, the door opened and in slinked a young woman. She was slightly over five feet tall and wore a tiny skirt that displayed slim bronze things. She was petite but very shapely and the dreadlocks that extended to the middle of her back gave her an exotic flair.

Most men shot her a quick glance when she walked in and then turned their attention back to the speaker. Not Daryl aka Player D. He was a true dick head. The type of man who thinks with his dick and not his head. It had always gotten him in all sorts of trouble but being Black mob connected always got him out of it; except for today.

Instead of paying attention to the meeting, Player D was paying homage to the girl's leopard-printed panties as she sat wide legged in a chair across the room. She saw him looking and licked her tongue at him. Dumb ass licked back and got smacked.

"I called your name five times Mr. Daryl but you are far more concerned with what's between Yolo's legs than in your own city!" Casper barked. "Is that why your receipts are so low lately?"

"No." Daryl lied as he raised his hand to his face. In fact, pussy or the pursuit of pussy was exactly why his money was short.

Player D was a big trick. He had at least ten known baby mommas in his hometown of Orlando. That's not counting his wife, his side piece, and a stable of hookers, hoes, strippers and jump offs. The majority of his time was spent dealing with his women and the drama they brought. He tricked lavishly on them all, spending more money than he had. If not for his second command, T-Rock, the business would be completely bankrupt. It was T-Rock who had salvaged what he could and reported what he couldn't. That's why he was invited to the meeting. He was about to get a promotion.

"If Yolo were to say...suck your dick, would that help you concentrate?" Casper asked with a murderous mirth that Player D missed.

"You know what?" The idiot nodded while every other man in the room sent him telepathic signals to shut the fuck up. "That probably would help. A nigga a lil up tight."

"Yolo take our guest into the playroom and suck his dick." Casper ordered.

"Mmmm." Yolo moaned in anticipation and stood up. A seductive smile spread on her exceptionally pretty face, making her look even younger than her twenty-one years. Player D took her hand as she led him off to slaughter. The other men in attendance only shook their heads morbidly, knowing he would next be seen at his wake. A few wondered how he survived this long.

Once the couple stepped from the boardroom, they made a left and walked halfway down the long carpeted hallway. Player D still held the petite hand but lagged back enough to watch her hips sway melodically. "Yolo? Short for Yolander?"

"In here." Yolo said, speaking for the first time as she opened a door. She led him into a nicely appointed guest room. Player D wasted no time dropping his pants and falling on the bed.

"If you suck it good enough, I'll let you ride it too." He announced generously.

"Would you?" Yolo exclaimed excitedly. That would be a first since Yolo was a virgin.

Well, it wouldn't be a first because it wasn't going to happen.

Yolo stepped out of the tiny skirt and pulled the shirt over her dreads. Her hard little breast needed no bra so none was present. The leopard-printed panties fit like a second skin, clearly showing a plump vagina underneath. She knealt at the foot of the bed and grabbed the now rock hard dick in her little hand.

"Ouch." Player D whined as Yolo bit the head sharply. She giggled girlishly and planted kisses all over it making him forget about the pain; until she did it again, that is.

Yolo bit then kissed him causing both pleasure and pain. Finally she took him as deep as she could into her mouth and sucked him slowly. Player D looked down and watched proudly as he slid in and out of her mouth. Men love that shit. He finally leaned back to enjoy getting sucked off. Yolo still bit him from time to time causing him to look down.

"Shit!" Player D winced from a dull pain more extreme from previous ones. He looked up and saw Yolo was still sucking his dick but something was off.

That's when he realized, she was standing up. He looked down to where his dick should have been just in time to see an arch of blood skeet with his heart beat. Yolo giggled still sucking the severed dick as panic set in.

"The fuck!" Player D screamed as he grabbed his crotchless crotch. He attempted to stop the bleeding but a river of red ran through his fingers. It dawned on him that if he got his dick back, he could put it back on. He lunged for Yolo to retrieve it but she scampered away.

"I used to be scared of the dick. Now I throw lips to the dick!" Yolo rapped into the dick like it was a microphone.

Player D chased her around the room losing blood, energy, and life with every beat of his heart. He almost had her when he grabbed a handful of dreads. Yolo shook her head and slipped out of the wig revealing her short, curly blonde hair underneath. He frowned at how heavy the wig was and tossed it aside with a dense thud.

The man eventually ran out of steam when he ran out of blood. He collapsed onto the floor with the look of utter heartbreak etched on his face. His eyes batted a few times as he blinked death into view. Having no other choice, he let go and went towards the light. The room, the man, and the killer were all covered in blood. The strong coppery smell would make most men gag but Yolo loved it. When she was finished playing in the blood, she put the man's dick in his pocket and slipped into the adjacent bathroom. A hot shower removed all the blood from the girl as she masturbated. Murder always made her horny. She dressed in a robe and stepped over the man as she left.

"Oh and Yolo isn't short for Yolander. It means, 'You Only Live Once.'" She finally answered the curious corpse.

When Yolo returned to the boardroom, no one was surprised to see her return alone. Casper was just wrapping up the pep talk/ass chewing.

He praised a few, slapped a few and spit on two before it was over with. As usual, the Baron never said a word. In fact, he barely even blinked.

"Okay, now everybody out! Go home and get to work!" Casper barked clearing the room in seconds.

The dangerous men held their tongues until they got outside. There they murmured and griped as they got into their expensive cars to head home. Once the room was cleared, except Baron and Yolo, Casper sauntered over to the throne-like seat of the Baron and looked up at him.

"Get the fuck out of my chair!"

Chapter 8

How a white man becomes the leader of the notorious Black Mob is an interesting story. Casper was born Mario Puzelli in the mobbed up Brighton Beach section of Brooklyn, New York. He was half Italian and half Irish but inherited his mother's pasty translucent white skin. It was the skin-tone that earned him the nickname Casper.

His half Italian blood earned him half entry into one of the neighborhood crews. It was comprised of all the teens he grew up with. The pack of thieves were as thick as thieves. They made their bones by pulling little capers and paid tribute up to the bosses for the right to earn and the privilege of breathing. Breathing is good.

By mid-twenties, all of his crew got made and were full members of the mob. Even though Casper was the brains behind the crew, his half Irish blood prevented him entry. He was a distant cousin in a band of brothers. Drug-dealing was strictly forbidden by the bosses. It earned well but too messy. Picture these proud people allowing their women to be whores, selling their souls and bodies for a hit; turning their own blocks into war zones with zombies roaming around. No, too messy. Let the niggers have it; they don't love themselves.

Casper had no love for black people either so he let them move all the drugs. It meant less money but far less heat. Less money; less problems as opposed to mo-money; mo-problems.

Greed got the best of the rest of the crew and they all branched off into sub-sets, selling everything from marijuana to molly's, kush to coke, and everything in between. It was all good until the feds swooped in. One by one they all got popped and one by one they all pointed their fingers at Casper.

Casper was smart enough to never have drugs on hand or it could have been worse. He was charged with conspiracy just off the word of his friends. Snitching on him saved their butts from the pen and lives from the mob. Now Casper's butt was in danger from prison and life from the mob.

The smart man hired an even smarter lawyer who was able to haggle a five year sentence from the government. He copped out to the nickle and was shipped off to begin his bid.

Five years in the feds for a non-violent charge is usually a cake walk. A couple of years at a minimum security camp that resembled a college campus more than a prison. No fences, no gun towers, good food, easy time; should be a piece of cake except for Casper's racist attitude and big ass mouth.

Calling niggers nigga was not only socially acceptable in the racist section of Brooklyn he grew up in, it was encouraged. If a black man wandered too deeply into their neighborhood, they would get chased out or worse. He had absolutely no respect for black people and it was about to cost him his ass, literally.

The gateway into the federal prison system is a diagnostic center in middle Pennsylvania. Here new inmates underwent a battery of mental and physical health screenings and this was where you received your security level. That meant the difference between easy time at Club Fed and hard time at a dangerous penitentiary.

"State your name and I.D. number please, sir." A courteous and professional black officer asked.

"Deez" Casper replied, looking back at his new buddies hoping to impress them.

"Deez?" The officer asked with a curious frown.

"Yeah, Deez nuts moolie!" Casper cracked, cracking him and his friends up. He was a riot, this guy.

"Listen, we can do this the easy way or the hard way." The officer offered, still being polite and professional.

"I'll take it the hard way like your momma likes it!" Casper shot back and burst out laughing again.

"My mother?" The officer asked with a pained expression on his face.

"Yeah, you momma, the black whore. Whoa!" He replied to delight his friends.

"My dear, sweet, deceased mother." The officer said softly. Her funeral was only days ago and the salt in the open wound stung. He was far more hurt than angry but still decided to get even.

Officer Black changed his security level from minimum to high. It meant the difference of baking bread in Bakersville and getting his salad tossed in Toledo. It would eventually get fixed but would it be in time to save his virginity is the question.

Casper was a big shot in the diagnostic center with his exaggerated mob ties. Since he really did live on the outskirts of that life, he was about to tell lies that sounded true. Word of the mobbed up Irish man spread far and wide. Spread all the way to Brooklyn.

****

"This must be some mistake." Casper said in near panic. The housing assignments of the next stage were passed out and he was not pleased.

While all his buddies were headed to various federal country clubs, Casper was headed to Passitville Penitentiary; more affectionately known as Ass-fuck-ville. Everyone familiar with the place clinched their butt cheeks at the very mention of the place.

"Shit, sucks to be you pizan. Don't drop the soap." One of his buddies laughed.

"He'll be aight. He's been around the cock...eeeh. I mean, block a few times." Another joked, showing the true friend they really were.

They all yucked it up real good except Casper who was terrified. His bung hole was in grave danger and he had to save it. He dug out his transcript and sentencing report to show there was some mistake.

"No problem" An officer relayed once he scanned the documents. "Simple fix. Just holler at Officer Black in the morning. He'll get you straight."

"Officer Black? The Black Guy?" Casper groaned as his disrespect circled around and slapped him. "Is there anyone else?"

"Nah, He's your man. Nicest guy you ever wanna meet. Poor fella. His mom just passed a few weeks ago"

The next morning Officer Black wore his throwback 'how you like me now' face as the contrite racist begged for his booty hole. Casper was so humble he barely recognized him from weeks earlier. Luckily for Casper, that same mother he so thoroughly disrespected raised her son right. He was compassionate, caring and did not hold grudges.

"I'll fix it in the computer but it'll take a few weeks to go through." The officer said as he typed the correction into the system.

"Weeks? What am I going to do for a couple of weeks?" Casper screamed.

"I can't tell you what you should do but I can tell you what not to do. Don't drop the soap; hold on tight to it, for dear life." Officer Black offered, fighting a smile and losing.

****

Casper was as scared as anyone who has been in any scary situation but he didn't let it show. He reverted back to his 'tough Italian mob guy' swagger as soon as he got off the bus.

He was from Brooklyn after all and he was connected. Add the fact that he didn't rat and that should count for something. The federal prosecutors offered him the world to turn snitch on the bosses but he refused. Instead he took his charges on the chin and accepted his fate.

He did his old ditty bop into the dorm as if it were the pizza shop back home. Casper nodded 'what's up' to his whites and scowled at the blacks. When he saw a group of obvious Italians, he made his way over to them to introduce himself before even going to his assigned cell.

"Say Pizan. Tell whoever one of you who runs the show, that Casper's here. Casper from Brooklyn. I'm a friend of you'se. Ask about me." He demanded as if in a position to make them. He swaggered away as arrogantly as he came, leaving the Italians confused.

"Casper from Brooklyn?" One asked. "What are we posed to do?"

"Shit, call Brooklyn, I guess." Came the reply complete with a shoulder shrug.

"Well, you'se guys better hurry. Look at whose cell he's in!" Another called out urgently.

B.B. was Casper's new bunk mate. He was six foot four inches of mass murderer from Mississippi. BB was an acronym for Black Bear because he looked like one. The only thing he liked about white people was killing them. Well, there was one thing more thing that he had developed in prison.

If there was a black people's equivalent to KKK, he would be its president. His baby sister was raped and killed by some racist back home and he killed every last one of them. It got good to him, so he killed a few more. That's what got him all the life sentences he was serving. He was warned he would get the death penalty if he killed one more white guy; so he stopped. Now he just fucks them. Makes love, have him tell it.

"Look it Moolie!" Casper announced as he barged into the cell. He had been in character so long; he actually started to believe it.

BB frowned at both the interruption as well as the slanderous remark. The word Moolie came from a dark purple eggplant. That's what black people were to him, eggplants; fucking vegetables.

"I'm Casper, from Brooklyn." He said, adding the Brooklyn part like it meant something. Now had he said the Bronx maybe. "I'm mobbed the fuck up, so don't fucking fuck with me!"

Poor BB didn't know what to think. On one hand, if he was truly a made man, he would be off limits. Prison had rules. If one wants to live, he must live by them. Then on the other hand, the way his lips moved during his rant had his dick hard. While he contemplated, an Italian stuck his head in the cell.

"Hey, we just spoke to Vito in Brooklyn." He huffed from running to relay the information.

"Tell this nigger who I'm with." Casper nodded, crossing his arms across his chest like a big shot.

"Well, you didn't check out, so I guess you're with him." The runner said, pointing at BB with his head. He shrugged his scrawny shoulders like 'oh well' and turned to leave.

BB's dick got so hard so quick, he was temporarily blinded. By the time his vision came back, Casper was gone. He spent the rest of his day on a call to Brooklyn, begging for protection. Because he violated the no drug policy, and. he wasn't a full member, he was on his own. He stayed away from the cell all day but when lockdown time came, he had no choice but to return. He decided to man up and apologize, forgive and forget.

"Lookit, I think we got off..." Casper began as he walked into the cell. The sight of the naked black man glistening from baby oil stole his train of thought.

"There's the pretty white girl I told you about." BB told his massive erection. If the man talking to his dick wasn't bad enough, it was worse when it seemed to nod at him; even winked its one eye.

What happened next was a classic example of the phrase 'from bad to worse.' When BB raped Casper that was bad but cuming in him was worse. The soft tender kisses and nibbles on the back of Casper's neck were bad but BB falling asleep on top and inside of him was worse.

Oh it was bad, lying there all night with a dick in your ass and its owner snoring loudly but feeling it grow hard inside of him that next morning was worse. And, oh, getting fucked again by a raging piss hard on was both bad and worse. He bust another nut with a loud grunt and more kisses and finally pulled out of the man's body.

"Come on, let's get some chow babe." BB suggested, as he washed his dick in the sink. "They got beef links!"

Casper felt like shit already but when a fart sent cum running down his leg, he just cried. Wouldn't you? Sure you would. He staggered down the hallway in a daze towards the chow hall. All eyes were on him when he walked in. His fellow Italians looked at him with scorn and disgust.

BB and his crew looked lustfully as he loudly recounted last night's events. He dubbed it a night in Casper and his buddies wanted in.

"What's the head like?" One of his buddies asked, as Casper walked pass with his beef links.

Casper decided just then to hang himself. Fuck it. Dead would have to be better than gang rape. Being passed around like a whore. Passed around like a blunt or a forty ounce amongst the niggers. Niggers were bad in general but inside of you; bad to worse; way worse.

"Here you go sir." Casper croaked as he handed his breakfast to an inmate sitting at a table by himself.

The Baron, as he was called was usually the largest man in any room, any time he stepped in any room. He was nearing the end of a bid for manslaughter for literally pulling a man's head off. In his whole bid, he never spoke and never had a friend. The offer of extra food for a person who had never been given anything was a life changing event. Plus it was beef links. He didn't speak but the look of appreciation in his cold eyes spoke volumes.

"Yeah, yeah, you'se welcome." Casper replied to the non-verbal thanks and moved on.

His life flashed before his eyes as he headed towards his death.

A slow rage began to simmer as he walked. It reached a rolling boil as he recounted abuse, betrayal and disrespect. By the time he reached his cell, he wanted to kill more than die. He wanted to kill BB for raping him. He wanted to kill the Italians for betraying and abandoning him. A thought of starting his own crew lifted his spirits but the next words he heard crashed them against he rocky shore.

"Hey pretty lady. This is my buddy Gene." BB said as he returned to the cell with a friend. The look in their eyes killed his dreams of a dick-free day.

"Wow, she is pretty." Gene gushed lustfully as he rubbed a sizable bulge in his pants.

Casper knew he couldn't fight them both so he turned and ran right into big Man, who was just coming in. Big Man liked pretty white girls too and had a bag full of canteen items to spend a little time.

"Whoa lil momma." Big Man cooed softly as he wrapped Casper in his big arms. That was bad, the tender kiss he planted on his trembling lips was worse.

Casper's thoughts again turned to suicide as the men began to strip him and themselves. He felt like he was stuck in the middle of a petrified forest with all the big wood surrounding him. He was easily forced to his knees despite his valiant efforts. The men slapped his face and popped his head playfully with their penises: Prison foreplay.

"Open up." Gene ordered, as he steered his erection in his direction. It was an inch away before being snatched from view.

"What th...." was all Gene could get out before being tossed into a wall so hard it required a nap.

This ain't none of none of your concern Baron." Big Man barked. He made a foolish step toward the man and took a short brutal beating that left him snoring. B.B felt obligated to fight and got the same. It was nap time in that cell.

Chapter 9

Killa grew antsy as months passed between jobs. Being couped up for so long made him restless. He needed to get out, move around, needed to murder something.

He didn't complain much since he had Kitty's pretty Kitty to entertain him. During vagina breaks, he researched all the pedophiles from the pastor's phone. He even traded text messages with a few. The disgusting pictures they shared, traded and sold only heightened Killa's desire to kill them all.

He planned to hunt them all down and murder them separately until he figured out a way to kill them all together. The next meeting of their secret society was coming up soon. In that next meeting they would meet their newest member, Xavier Forrest. Sure, it was dangerous using his real name, especially since the members included police, lawyers, judges and clergy. But, not one of the men would live past that next meeting to tell about it.

Finally, after watching and checking his work phone, it rang. Killa felt a mix of elation and loathing as he picked up the cellular device.

"You ready to get back to work?" The voice asked curtly when Killa took the call. He literally had to bite his tongue so he would be able to bite it figuratively. He loathed the sarcastic undertones always present in the voice.

"Sure, whatcha got?" Killa replied stoically.

"Oh, we go a couple of guys who desperately need dead; real pieces of shit. Please kill them. The client can't decide on a manner of death so you have free reign. Only, be creative because the client wishes to view."

"When and where?" Killa asked eagerly. He loved his job. Love to travel to new cities and meet new people and then kill them.

"As soon as possible and its local, Metro Atlanta. Not too far from you?" The voice offered.

"Nah, not too far." Killa replied, satisfied with the question mark at the end of the statement. It meant they still didn't know his exact whereabouts.

When Killa came aboard with the Black Mob, he was given a company car and a condo in downtown Atlanta. The car was a new luxury job with all the bells and whistles including a GPS tracker to keep track of his whereabouts. Likewise, the condo was loaded with cameras and recording devices. Killa drove Kitty to the condo and fucked the daylights out of her for the camera before abandoning them both. He came across his secluded hideaway and the couple set-up shop.

The place where Killa laid his head was an hour's drive north of Atlanta. It was modest, handsomely appointed but best of all, secluded. Set off the road kept it free from prying eyes and burying the real estate agent in the back meant his lips were sealed; casualty of war. Some people have to die so that others can live in peace.

At the termination of the call, a file was sent on the two future victims. By the time Killa reviewed it, he felt like calling back and offering his services for free. These two dudes definitely needed killing and it was going to be brutal.

****

"Your honor, we plan to appeal this verdict!" Public defender, David Queen boomed at the judge.

"Appeal all you want, the jury has spoken." Assistant District Attorney Bob Sheats taunted. The two court room adversaries faced each other and verbally attacked.

They put on another trial right there on the floor, arguing flaws and errors. All eyes and attention were turned to the two men.

"Order! Order in my court." The ancient judge barked, simultaneously banging his gavel. "You have thirty days to file an appeal. Now clear my courtroom!"

"Don't worry; we'll beat in on appeal." Queen said, turning to face his shocked client.

"But, I'm innocent. I didn't rob a store." The young black man said just above a whisper. His nightmare of being falsely accused of a liquor store robbery had just gotten worse when he was wrongly convicted. "What happened to all my witnesses? I was with all those people, at church."

"Uh.....well...we uh couldn't locate..didn't get a cha....we'll beat in on appeal." Queen stammered as the bailiff came to collect the prisoner.

Soft moans and low wails were heard from the defendant's family as he was shackled and led away. Queen again assured them that he could get the case overturned during the appeals' process. One-by-one the courtroom emptied until all that remained was the opposing lawyers.

The public defender and district attorney glared at each other as they loaded their briefs and paperwork back into attaché cases. They both stood erect and walked up on each other, mean mugging. Slowly their scowls became smiles.

"Dun dun dun, another one bites the dust." They laughed and sang together.

High fives and chest bumps were next to follow then a hug so tight, someone should have said 'no homo' but no one did.

"So, are we celebrating tonight?" The crooked D.A. asked the public pretender.

"But of course!" Queen cheered. It had been their ritual for the last twenty years to go out and celebrate each time they railroaded another black man.

Queen and Sheats had been sending innocent men to prison for twenty years. Even though Queen was black himself, he still had a hatred of black men. He felt they were an embarrassment. He would just lie down and not challenge anything the state presented.

In this case, his client was a college student home for the weekend. He was returning from a church social when pulled over by police and arrested. There were hundreds of people who could have confirmed his whereabouts; including pictures and video but they lawyer suppressed it all. It more than likely would be reversed somewhere down the line but he was going to prison for now.

The dastardly duo would leave their ugly, loveless wives at home for a romp with a stripper. For years, they had used the service of a pimp named Mitch to supply them with girls, drugs and a place to party.

Mitch had been selling pussy in Atlanta for as long as anyone could remember. He once had the market cornered with a stable of whores that resembled a U.N. meeting. Younger and more aggressive pimps rose to power and staked claims to what Mitch had built. They put their own girls on his tracks and disrespectfully recruited his girls. He was on his way out to pasture until joining the black mob. When he got the call to supply the party favors, he got everything in order: Champagne, weed and of course a woman. He sent a new girl but she was no hooker.

Killa pulled up to the rented villa and checked his gear. This job didn't require much of anything since he had carte blanch to do as he wanted. All the client requested was to be heard before the deed and to be able to witness the execution. He had one more thing in mind of his own.

Mitch had supplied a key to the villa which allowed the killer to enter easily and quietly. The front room was empty but a ruckus could be heard from the back. Killa raised a silencer-equipped nine millimeter and followed his ears.

"The fuck?" Killa exclaimed in curious disgust as he entered the bedroom.

The two men were both butt naked, engaged in a masturbation race while a sinister looking prostitute cheered them on. They were far more concerned with the race than the man with the gun.

"Um...excuse me." Killa said with a grimace. He hit the power button on the sereo and killed the music.

"Hey!" I was about to win! The public defender protested.

"No, I win!" The D.A. grunted as he crossed the finish line.

"You, out!" Killa demanded to the girl on the bed. She frowned in a manner that forced Killa to remember the instructions to let the girl go. Still, he didn't like the look she gave him.

The young woman shipped her dreadlocks onto her back and stood. Killa could not help but admire the firm body and pretty face. She stepped into a tiny dress then onto a pair of stilettos. She never broke off her glare until she left the room.

"Don't look so tough to me." Yolo huffed as she exited the villa.

"What's the meaning of this?" The D.A. barked, as if he were in control. A back hand slap with the pistol opened a gash in his forehead. "Hey! I'm placing you under citizen's arrest! Put the gun down and hands in the air."

"Is this dude serious?" Killa asked his partner in crime before slapping him again. This blow from the gun got his full attention.

"What do you want from us?" Queen pleaded. He sounded just like those clients of his who pleaded for their freedom.

"Me, nothing, but someone would like to have a word with you." Killa replied as he retrieved his phone and pulled up the client's message.

"David Queen and Bob Sheats. It's been a long time." The female's voice stated. She tried to sound tough, like she was in control but the pain was visible just under the surface.

"Fifteen years ago you had my father, Emory Teasly in your court. His life was in your hands and you betrayed him. I sat t here and watched my daddy get convicted of a murder committed while we had a cookout. You sold him out, didn't call a single witness. Well, my daddy died in the death chamber last week. Today, you join him."

Queen and Sheats looked at each other in fear. They remembered the case vividly. They knew they went too far in convicting him. They covered their tracks to save their own asses.

"So what now, you, kill us?" Sheats demanded.

"No, I'm only going to kill one of you. I'll let you guys decide who. But first" Killa paused to set-up the recorder on his phone. "I need a confession. It may save lives."

The men misunderstood whose life it could save and candidly recounted sending innocent men up the river for decades. In the recording, they attempted to shift blame back and forth to help themselves. The confession did save their lives, but only for the hour it took to give.

"Well, time for one of you guys to die. Who gets it?" Killa asked nonchalantly.

"Him!" They both shouted, pointing trembling fingers at each other. Killa couldn't help but laugh at their treachery. They wasted no time in turning on each other.

"Like I said, you guys decide who lives." Killa repeated. He pulled two butcher knives from his bag and handed one to each man. They didn't hesitate a millisecond before attacking each other.

"Fuck!" Killa giggled as they viciously attacked each other. He had to scramble to start the recording the client requested.

Neither attorney had any defense; they just stabbed and got stabbed. The room was splattered with blood as arteries and blood vessels were ruptured. The action began to slow as the combatants ran out of steam and blood. They both thrust a final blow into each other and collapsed.

Killa pumped a couple of rounds into the back of each man's head as he prepared to leave. Once he was satisfied that all traces of his presence had been removed, he made his exit.

"Well, that was fun." Killa chuckled to himself as he pulled away.

Chapter 10

"Okay." A nervous CSI tech whispered signaling the arrival of the Chief of Police. The top cop commanded awe in general, but lately he had become a monster.

Chief Flores stepped from his government car, cowboy boot first, like the cowboy that he was. It was rumored that back in the day when he was just a cop, he was on a death squad. Jail, court, lawyers all cost money. For certain crimes suspects were executed rather than arrested.

"What do we have?" He questions when he ascertained who was in charge of the crime scene. He did not speak to underlings.

"It's another one." The lead detective said meekly. By 'another one' he meant another headless girl. Another one, just like the Chief's daughter. The fifth such find of the year. If the scene wasn't grisly enough, the question that twisted the policemen's faces was, 'where the fuck are the heads.'

The chief looked down upon the mangled corpse and shook his head. He had to blink away the vision of his own child's dismembered body. In America, he would not have been allowed to even work the case. Down here, they couldn't stop him. It was well-known there would be no trial for this one. Whoever caught the elusive suspect was to hold him until the chief arrived. He had no interest in a trial or justice. All he wanted now was tow things: His daughter's head back and the head of whoever killed her. A commotion behind the yellow tape snapped him from his vengeful thoughts and he went to investigate.

"Que pasa?" Chief demanded, as a hysterical woman rambled in rapid fire Spanish to the pee-on officer assigned to crowd control.

"This woman claims to know who is doing this!" I told her to leave and let the police do their jobs." He said smugly.

The chief's first words were a back-hand slap that was universal in all languages. In the inner cities, it's what's known as a pimp slap.

58

"Talking to the people is police job stupid." He yelled, stinging him just as much as the slap. His tone softened as he turned to the woman. "Who is doing this?" He asked soothingly.

"The gringo doctor from the village! The American!" She replied eagerly. She had been desperately warning the people about the man every since her own granddaughter went missing. The villagers didn't want to hear anything bad about the man who provided free medical care. Not to mention, the girl was a known slut; a disposable woman.

"Is this him?" Chief Flores demanded, producing surveillance pictures of Doc from the hotel.

"Si, si!" She screamed at the sight of him. She looked directly in the cops flaming red eyes and nodded. "This is the man."

****

Costa Rica is a beautiful place; God country as they say. As if they don't know everything in existence is His. He created; He shaped it and maintains it. Its tiny stretches of land contained jungles and forests, waterfalls and volcanoes. God's country indeed.

It was good for more than just killing, so Doc got out and explored the sights. He had been surfing, para-surfing and snorkeling. Today he was flying over an active volcano on a sight-seeing tour. The next stop was a huge waterfall where rainbows lived. At the same moment Doc snapped a picture with his camera, his door came off its hinges.

Chief Flores personally kicked the doctor's door open and rushed inside with an assault rifle. The rest of his officers fell back as he stormed the villa. No one even had any handcuffs but there was a body bag on hand.

The chief had so much pressure on the trigger of his gun that a blink of an eye would have been enough to discharge it. Each time he entered a room, he made a silent prayer that the killer be inside of it.

Murder has a taste, both bitter yet sweet and it was present on the cop's tongue.

"Clear!" He finally said, feeling dejected once he accepted that the villa was empty. He plopped down on the sofa as the rest of the team swarmed the house.

The house was a buzz in a flurry of activity as CSI techs and detectives rummaged about. They turned the small house upside down and inside out in a search for clues; in cabinets, under beds and dressers; in closets and crawl spaces, even the attic. The attic, that's where they found them.

The chief was immune to the sounds of the search and paid it no mind. It wasn't until the place grew eerily quiet that his head lifted from his hands. The solemn silence sounded like mourning. It was; Bonita had been found. He noticed everyone whispering and going up to the attic. He noticed their faces were different when they came back down so he went to investigate.

"Chief, I don't think you should...." An officer warned, attempting to prevent him from going up. Again with the back-hand like Venus Williams.

Everyone fled the attic once chief arrived. In the attic, there was a shelf. On the shelf there were jars. In the jars there were heads. Each head was perfectly preserved down to the disappointed looks on their faces. All the girls looked sad especially his daughter. The chief plucked the jar containing the missing part of his only child from the shelf and sat down. The proud man broke down in sobs and low wails.

All the police were affected by the grisly find, some more than others. One CSI tech who didn't quite have the stomach for it, ran to the edge of the property to relieve the bubbling bile from his stomach. As he retched over the cliff, something caught his eye. Some things actually: More bodies.

"Oyay!" He screamed and pointed to the vultures feeding below.

"Adios Mio!" His comrade exclaimed and crossed himself as his binoculars revealed what was on their menu. There were ten or more bodies below.

This was now a full blown crime scene. More techs had to be called in along with the National Guard to retrieve the bodies. The small country had never dealt with anything like this before. All the activity alerted the media and in turn the media alerted the Doc.

Doc was actually on his way home w hen he saw emergency and government vehicles rushing past. The helicopters hovering above made him pull a u-turn that allowed him to miss the check point being set-up just for him.

Doc was a smart man doing dumb shit and he knew he could be caught at any moment. That kept him on point and prepared to flee at the drop of a dime. Any time he left the house, he carried a money belt and travel documents. He raced south, heading to the Panama border and safety. He had found out that one of his victims was the daughter of the police chief and ran for his life.

Using forged documents, he crossed the border as a tourist. A long bus ride later, he arrived in Panama City. There was no time to see the world famous canals. His destination was the airport. Doc was coming to America.

Chapter 11

Big Rock was one of the biggest dealers in the city of Baltimore; both physically and figuratively. The six-foot five-inch ex-ball player controlled the cities coke trade. B-more is a heroine city but still had a bustling blow trade. The black mob accepted that it would be too much trouble trying to break into the heroine market. There were too many free agents to contend with and despite Yolo's contention, you can't kill everyone.

Big Rock already had a nice operation going when the black mob made its offer. A classic get down or lay down offer you can't refuse. Sell their blow and live or die and someone else would sell it. He chose to live; smart choice.

It was all good until the Mendez Brothers came to town. The black Puerto Ricans moved in with their superior grade coke and low prices and the impact was felt immediately. Once they got a toe-hold in the city, they wouldn't let go. They wisely recruited locals and paid them twice what they had been making. Make no mistake about it, loyalty is for sale. That's why a woman will stay with a man who cheats and treats them bad if the money is right. Talk about sell outs!

Big Rock being the killer that he was, sent men to kill the intruders but they always came up empty. Either the brothers killed them or hired them. A couple of times, they sent the same killers back at Big Rock. After they killed his best man, the mob decided to send in a girl.

Gabby and Pedro Mendez were freaks, straight tricks. They made their headquarters in a strip club named 'The Body Tap.' This particular strip joint was known to have the baddest and freakiest chics in town. The brothers made it a point to fuck each and every one of them. So you know the new girl demanded their attention, especially doing what she was doing.

The exotic looking girl with dreads was regulated to one of the smaller side stages since she was new but all eyes were on her. It was more than the hard softball sized breast topped by big erect nipples that stood just above her rock-hard six pack. A small waist jetted out to a nice round ass under curvy hips. The dreadlocks obscuring her face added an air of mystery.

"A-yo son, look at this bitch right here!" Gabby practically screamed as he pointed to the slide stage.

"The fuck?" Pedro exclaimed and took to his feet. He and his brother drew near as in a trance. Pussy will do that, especially new pussy.

The girl was causing quite a scene and she wasn't even dancing. Instead, she sat Indian-style making circles on her love button with her finger.

"Get the fuck out of the way." Tank demanded, shoving patrons out of his bosses' path.

The brothers made it to the stage just in time for her to bust a shuddering nut. The gush of juice that dripped when she came sealed the deal, as it should have.

"A-yo, go tell Steve, we taking this bitch with us." Pedro said to Tank.

"Yo shorty, get dressed." Gabby told her, talking to her vagina instead of her face.

"Ok." She purred naively and stood up. She walked slightly wobbly on her six inch heels still shaky from the orgasm. In a flash she returned from the dressing room wearing only slightly more than when she left. The tiny dress only blinked her nakedness away.

"Steve ain't answering his door or phone." Thank repeated when he returned from his task. He had a disappointed look on his face from not being able to complete his task. The large man had the mind of a small child and loved to please.

"Aight yo, stay here until you find him." Gabby ordered over his shoulder.

"Ain't like we need security for this chic." Pedro laughed, as they pushed the girl from the club. "What's yo name lil mama?"

"Yolo" She replied with the lustful look of a lunatic.

The Mendez Brothers rushed to their waterfront loft with the killer in the back seat, still playing in her pussy. She made a small puddle on the leather underneath her when she came again. Pedro pulled into the underground parking lot and skidded to a stop in their reserved spot. He barely put it in park before Gabby sprang free and snatched Yolo from the back seat. Pedro reached back and put his finger in the puddle and into his mouth with his nasty ass.

Yolo's feet barely touched the ground as the brothers rushed her up to their unit. She looked around the plush living room in search of items to use as weapons. Besides her specially made stilettos, she was completely un-armed. Gun or no gun, Yolo was dangerous as fuck. The dudes were about to die from blunt force trauma. That means getting beat to death.

"Heads or tails?" Pedro announced as he flicked a quarter turning it n the air.

"Heads!" Gabby called out watching it ascend and descend. He wanted first inside of her mouth. He, like a lot of men, this author included was a head junky. Someone needs to make a patch for that, a re-hab or support group or.....

"Heads it is!" Pedro lied when the coin toss came back tails. He wanted to fuck her first so he gave his brother what he wanted.

An unseen and unheard starter pistol was fired and the race to get naked was under way. Yolo won easily since all she had to do was drop the straps from her shoulders and let the flimsy dress fall to the ground. Both brothers snatched off their designer jeans and boxers in one swift motion. Shirts were pulled over heads and they were as naked as their guest. Their erections bobbed in the air as they moved on her.

Yolo didn't complain when she was shoved roughly onto the sofa. She figured why complain since she was going to murder them anyway.

Gabby rushed over and pressed his dick against her lips. She took the head inside her mouth as she popped the balls off the heels of her stilettos, revealing the super sharp dagger like ends. When Pedro pulled her legs sky high to enter her, she thrust them at his face. The knives entered both eyes just as she clamped down on the dick head with her teeth.

Pedro screamed and grabbed where his eyes use to be and stumbled back. He tripped on the glass table and fell through it, shattering the glass. His screams were nothing compared to the high pitched ones of his brother.

"Yeeooow!" Gabby belted out an opera worthy note. Yolo covered up like a boxer against the ropes and he wailed away with heavy blows, trying to dislodge her from his penis.

It was to no avail because she had locked on like a pit bull. She wrapped her arms around his waist as he flopped around to shake her off. He finally got free when her teeth met all the way through his meat. If he had a horse, he could now be called the Headless Horseman. Ok, that may not have been funny but it was when she spit it at him.

"Here!" Yolo said through her bloody smile when his dick head bounced off his chest. When he went for it, she went for the heavy glass ashtray on an end table.

"Bitch I'mma...."

"Ugh!" Yolo grunted as she swung the ashtray. The blow knocked the threat back down his throat along with several of his teeth.

She beat him unmercifully until he dropped to one knee. His head lowered in front of her like an offering and she took him up on it. Yolo swung with all her might and split his wig and cracked his skull. You could put a fork in him because he was done.

"You don't look so good." She teased Pedro as he wallowed in the broken glass.

"Fuck you!" Gabby, kill this bitch!" He yelled for his brother who couldn't hear shit. Well maybe harps.

"Uh uh, the bitch killed Gabby." She laughed, giving him a stomp that stabbed into a lung. It got good to her so she stomped him again. Finally she mounted him and jumped up and down with her deadly high heels. She stopped about a minute after his heart did.

"That was fun." She gushed looking around to bloody room. She didn't even bother to clean the blood from her before slipping back into the dress. On the way out, she blew out the pilot light on the gas fireplace and turned the gas on high. When the condo was full of gas fumes, the pilot light in the stove would do the rest.

Yolo fished out the keys to her new Benz from Pedro's pocket and left. She was several blocks away when the orange explosion shook the night. The blast was large enough to destroy all units next to it along with their sleeping occupants.

****

Back at the club, Tank was still guarding Steve's door, waiting for him to return. It was futile because there was no coming back from where Yolo sent him. Earlier in the day, she came in and asked about dancing in the club so she could get close to her targets. She could dance and had no problem auditioning for the job. It could have been simple until his dick came out.

"Look shawty, I ain't got time for you to be prancing yo lil ass 'round my office. Let me see what that dome talking 'bout." He said, waving his dick at her.

"You want some head huh?" She asked, coming around his desk for a reply. He leaned back and handed it to her. A minute later, she handed it back.

"What the fuck is th....." He started to protest until Yolo shoved one of her spiked stilettos into his throat. Death has a way of ruining a conversation. Who really feels like talking once they're dead?

Ever faithful and obedient, there's no tell how long Tank would have stayed at that door. If Steve's angry wife wouldn't have shown up, he may have stood there all night.

"Where the hell is my husband?" She demanded, staring up at Tank.

"Uh he aint in there." Tank said, frightened by the small woman with the huge fake breast.

Steve's wife, Ava was a textbook plain Jane until he overhauled her. She had been down before he blew up and even trooped a bid with him. Instead of leaving her for one of the gold diggers that comes with the gold, he just customized her. He pimped his wife like Xibit pimps cars. The tiny titties were super-sized along with Botox, lipo and butt shots. She even had a pony tail made from a real pony's tail. It was called the Lil Kim package and just like Lil Kim, she looked better before than after.

"Why the fuck you standing guard for then!" Ava screamed, proving they haven't invented anything for a nasty mouth or fucked up attitude. "Get the fuck outta my way!"

Tank frowned down at the little woman beating on his big chest with her little hands. When he stepped aside, she fished around in her large designer purse until she hooked a lone key. She had it copied one night for an occasion just like this. The look on her face when it turned the lock was priceless but the once when she opened the door coast a little more.

"Steve!" Tank lamented at the sight of the manager propped at his desk.

His eyes were still wide from shock and his shirt and desk were covered in blood. The ragged hole in his throat explained where it came from. Tank and Ava inched cautiously into the office, glancing around to make sure the killer was gone. A lone tear escaped Ava's eye at the sight of her dead husband. When she saw his exposed penis, she knocked it away with a swift back hand.

"Uh huh!" Ava berated and she gave his stiff leg a stiff kick. Poor fellow was still getting chewed out in death. No rest for the weary. "Leave us alone for a few minutes before I call the police."

"Un, ok." Tank replied, confused. Not sure what he should be doing, he stepped out into the hall and called his bosses. Neither Mendez brother answered their phones because the signal doesn't go that far.

As soon as Tank cleared the room, Ava cleared the safe and then his pockets, wrist, fingers and neck. What? The police or paramedics would have stolen it if she didn't. The cash from the safe took several trips to move. Some of it belonged to the Mendez Brothers but they certainly wouldn't miss it.

Chapter 12

"Boy, why you ain't tell me you had a baby up here. I know I raised you better than that!"

"Whoa, whoa grandma. Slow down, what are you talking about?" Killa asked throwing his hands in surrender as if she could see him.

"Um, your little friend Sincerity? When is the last time you spoke with her?" Deidre huffed. Killa could see her in his mind, tapping her foot awaiting a response.

"Not since I was last up there when I got your stuff back for you." He said stifling a smile at the memories of that night.

The only thing better than killing the little bastard who stole from his family was killing the men who claimed to be God. The only thing better than that was the sex with Sincerity. His grandmother's next words wiped the smile from his handsome face.

"Mm hmm, and your ass made a baby! Now you better get up here and see your son!" She spat.

"Son? Grandma what in the world are you talking about? Do I need to call a nurse for you?"

"Here!" Deidre barked.

"Hello?" Sincerity asked weakly into the phone. Not weak from fear but weak from just giving birth.

"A-yo is my grandmother ok? What the hell is she talking about?" Killa asked causing Kitty to frown out of concern from his tone of voice.

"Uh...well?...um....ok....remember when you was up here and we did it? Well....you got a son." She finally admitted.

"......I'm on my way." Killa said and hung up.

"Is everything ok?" Kitty purred sympathetically. It was just that sort of concern that prevented him from following up on Sincerity. "You want me to come with you?"

Sure he fucked a few chics here and there when out of town killing; just dick, nothing serious. But Sincerity would have required more than that. She took emotions, heart and soul. These were things that belonged to his Kitty.

"Nah, some family shit. I'd better go alone." He replied, climbing out of bed.

"Family shit huh?" Kitty complained. She didn't complain much but lately she had been wanting more as love for him spread from her heart to her soul.

"I promise you'll meet my people soon." Killa said, wondering how to keep that promise.

"Thank you daddy!" Kitty cheered, smiling and clapping. "Yay! Cuz my momma coming soon and I want you to meet her!"

"That's fine." He agreed, even though it wasn't in his heart. Still, whatever wifey wants wifey gets.

"Now come on over here so I can give you a proper going away." She offered wickedly. Of course he said yes because men don't say no to head. Yes to head! Yes to head! Yes.....

****

Killa's journey home was dominated by thoughts of his son Xavier. He had been sole heir to the throne until now. He wasn't sure what to make of this new revelation. Sincerity was not the type to try him on some bullshit, so why would she not tell him about being pregnant. He couldn't come up with an answer, so he waited to pose it to her directly.

Before he knew it, he was creeping into the Bronx's Lincoln Hospital. The swift elevator delivered him to the maternity room quickly than he would have liked but there he was.

"Sincerity Jones?" Killa asked a pretty forty something nurse at the nurses' station. She flirted slightly, leaning forward, offering a glimpse of her ample chest along with the directions. Killa took her up on both, offering his smile as thanks.

"Sup?" Killa asked sheepishly, as he entered the room.

"Sup with choo?" Sincerity replied, glancing up from the bundle on her chest.

"Shit you tell me." He shot back and drew near. "My grandmother talk..." One look at the baby with its classic Forrest features stopped him short from finishing the question.

It was un-needed confirmation because Sincerity wasn't that chic. Her reputation in the projects, the borough and the city was flawless.

"So, why you ain't get at me? Why you ain't say anything?" Killa wondered, never averting his eyes from the infant.

"Nigga, I told you when you were here it was your move. I gave myself to you completely: The whole me, mind, body and soul. I guess you just wanted the pussy cuz that's all you took. You just left the rest; the best part." She said directly to his soul.

"Aight Ma, but why not tell me you was pregnant?"

"Killa, I'm pregnant!" Sincerity snapped like Sincerity does. "To keep it one hundred, I wasn't gonna say shit. I just happened to be checking on yo grandma when my water broke! I think ole girl knew all along cuz I kept catching her giving my belly the side eye! Anyway, meet Rico, your son."

"Rico?" Killa asked, pulling a mask of remorse over his face; just like a ski mask.

"Yeah, Rico. I hope you ain't mind. I ain't put it on the birth certificate yet. But don't worry, you won't have to kill him." She said soft and knowingly.

"When did you find out about that?" He asked, feeling a feeling closely related to embarrassment. Cousins maybe.

"Just now." You know the projects stay buzzing but your reaction to hearing my brother's name confirmed it." She replied.

"Do you wanna know why?"

"Nope. Don't care." Sincerity answered quickly. "I know my brother was some bullshit and when people speak of you they use words like crazy, sick, dangerous, but always loyal. Besides his death got my moms off drugs. She was fucked up on that shit until he died. His death saved her life, mine too. Can you imagine being the child of a crackhead?"

"Umm Yeah." Killa admitted, thinking about his own mother for the first time in a long time.

"Is everything ok?" A petite, pretty red-headed nurse asked as she breezed into the room.

"Yes, fine." Sincerity sang, smiling down proudly at her newborn. He was healthy as a little horse but the doctors wanted to keep them both overnight for observation due to the difficult birth. Little Rico came into the world feet first, just like his daddy.

Sincerity may have been smiling but Killa wasn't. He frowned that 'where do I know you from' frown at the familiar face. He had definitely seen this chic before. No question.

"That's great." The nurse gushed. "I'm Yolo....uh...landa. Yoldanda. Ask for me if you need anything."

"Here you are!" Deidra exclaimed as she entered the room. Killa and he nurse glared at each other as she made her exit.

"Hey grandma." He said, bracing himself for a hearty embrace. You know grandmothers give the best hugs. They can actually snap a child in half if not careful.

"Boy you know I got a bone to pick with you!" She warned, and then proceeded to pick it. Sincerity smiled brightly at the sight of the notorious killer getting chewed out.

After a thorough tongue lashing, Deidra took her grandson home to feed him. Have her tell it, he was skinny and malnourished. Good thing Kitty wasn't here to hear that because she would have wanted to fight. Two things she did do and did well was feed and fuck her man. He dined on world class Cajun fare for dinner and good ole Louisiana pussy for desert.

Killa returned to the hospital the next day to retrieve his family. He hoped to have enough time to search for the nurse who made him so uncomfortable. Not sure if she was a friend or foe. So, he was going to murder her anyway. You know, just in case. No such luck because Sincerity was waiting in the lobby with their son. She thrust the infant on him as soon as he walked in.

"So, what are we gonna do now?" Sincerity asked as they relaxed on her plush sofa. She wished she was able to fuck him first before asking, but at least she fed him. Men are much more pliable when full or fucked.

"We ain't gonna do nothing. Nothing changed. I'ma still take care of you like I always have." He said firmly.

"Not good enough." She demanded. "Look, I ain't telling you to leave her, whoever she is. I wouldn't. Besides, if that were an option, I know you would have done it already. All I'm saying is me too! You have two women now and I want what's mine! Don't worry, you can handle it."

"That's what's up." Killa agreed. It wasn't like he had much of a choice anyway.

A week after arriving in New York, it was time to leave. Killa was horny after a sexless week, since Sincerity's vagina was closed for repairs after childbirth. He had plans to come back for the grand re-opening in five weeks. Dick sucking is an acquired taste that Sincerity had yet to acquire, so he was desperate for his Kitty and her Kitty.

"The fuck?" Killa frowned as his business phone rang seconds after turning it back on in Atlanta. He had just stepped from the plane and it un-nerved him. He hated feeling like they knew his every step. They did.

"Yeah!" Killa barked into the phone.

"So, how was your trip?" The annoying voice asked.

"Shit you tell me!" He snapped, not even attempting to hide his disdain for the owner of the voice.

"Well considering that you didn't kill anyone this trip, I'd say it was a pretty good trip. At least daddy won't have to spank you." He laughed more to antagonize than mirth.

"Look here nigg....."

"Oh chillax! Don't get your panties in a bunch! I wouldn't want you to say something you may or may not live to regret. While you're in the airport, you may as well catch a flight out to California. I have a job for you, a domestic dispute. Same price."

"Aight yo. Send me flight info and target." Killa said as he literally bit his tongue to prevent what was on his mind from spilling out his mouth.

Chapter 13

Killa called ahead to one of his long time friends to meet him at LAX. Him and Big Cyke of the Shotgun Crips had been down since they were shooting people with 22s. Anytime he came to Cali to kill, they linked up and hung out. This time was no exception and the big homie met him at the plane. There was Cyke holding up a sign like the limo drivers only his said, Killa.

"Killa? Really?" He laughed and exchanged a pound and a hug from his friend.

"You know what I'm saying." Cyke replied in his deep, gravely voice, as if that were an answer.

"The Notorious Big Cyke!" Killa exclaimed proudly, looking over at his dude as they navigated their way out of the crowded airport. The sound of the expired moniker stopped the man dead in his tracks.

"Whoa homie, I ain't even on that no more cuz. I'm Muslim now. My name is Jihad." He said seriously.

"Jihad?" Holy war?" Killa asked ignorantly. It was an ignorance honed to a dull edge by slanderous, biased and slanted media reports.

"It don't mean holy war. How can any war ever be holy?" He shot back. "Jihad means to strive, to struggle and the greatest struggle is against your own self. What you think I just dropped my flag and went legit just like that? I mean, I did but it's still a struggle."

"Aight, so no more Crip walk?" Killa asked, twisting his lips dubiously.

"Well......sometimes when I'm in the crib alone." Jihad admitted, cracking them both up. "So, where you staying?" You know you're always welcome to crash with me."

"Nah, I'ma grab a room to make moves from but I'm spending the night at a woman's place." Killa replied.

"Sho nuff, got a chic out here?"

"No, I'll bag one from the club tonight." He shot back. "I do need some heat though."

"I told you I ain't 'bout that life no more....but I know a guy." Jihad laughed. He may not have been bout that life but he still had a 64 pancaked in the parking deck.

Killa tossed his bag in the back seat and climbed down into the passenger seat. Jihad crunk the pristine Chevy big block to life and hit the switches. The car bounced up to a drivable position and they were off. Another switch was hit and a small screen unfolded itself from the dash radio. Instead of Snoop and Dre's; G-Thang, the car filled with a melodic Qur'an recitation. Both men's hearts were at rest as they rode towards Gardenia.

After giving Killa the Islamic tour of Los Angeles, he took him by one of the homies to procure some L.A. sunshine, that heat, a burner. Jihad dropped his friend and his new gun off at a downtown hotel so he could rest from the trip.

"Shit" Killa panicked when the alarm snatched him from his sleep. He thought he had overslept but the three-hour time difference took up the slack.

He reluctantly rolled out of the plush bed and headed into the bathroom. After relieving himself, he stepped into the shower. Setting the custom shower head to pulsate he got a massage as he washed the traces of travel away. It was a half hour later when he finally pulled himself away. The ultra thick hotel towels literally sucked the water from his lean muscular body.

His gear for the night was slightly wrinkled so Killa set up the room ironing board. A few burst of steam knocked the wrinkles from his linen pants and Egyptian cotton shirt. A pair of gator loafers set the casual outfit off quite nicely. He looked down at his watch and nodded. It was a time to kill.

The car service provided by the hotel rode him in style through night time Los Angeles. It was no New York but it was cool. On the way to the club, he studied the file on his next victim. The pretty, blue-eyed woman had enjoyed her last sunset because she would not see sunrise.

The venue was a quaint mid-sized spot on Wilshire; upscale but casual, where jazz was played under dim lights. Killa squinted and blinked the place into focus as he strolled in with his killer swag. He quickly spotted his target minutes after entering. Not only was she just like she looked in the picture but she demanded attention.

The woman perched precariously a top a bar stool with one luscious leg crossed over the other. The tiny red dress made a sexy contrast against the tan thighs. It was the same color as the pumps on her manicured feet. The spaghetti straps kept falling off her shoulders threatening to expose one of the plump breasts it barely contained.

"Shit, I might fuck around and smash that before I kill her." Killa mused to himself as he approached.

He couldn't help but think how odd of a job this one was; not quite as odd as feeding a child molesting pastor to pigs but still odd none the less. Unlike the preacher, she actually had a choice to live or die. She could grab her purse, go home and live. She could pick any of the other hounds sniffing at her ass and live. There were several men offering dick donations to her feed the greedy foundation; the organization set-up for the benefit of her damn self. She could have but instead she leaned over and asked, "Do I know you?"

"You can." Killa replied, flashing his killer smile.

"I want you to come home with me." She demanded and prepared to leave. She uncrossed her legs deliberately wider and slower than necessary to give him a view of her shaved vagina.

Killa shrugged at her choice to die and followed her out. Once outside the valet rushed off to retrieve her chariot, and what a chariot it was. Moments later, he returned in a growling, headless V-12 Bentley.

"You drive!" She demanded, like a woman use to making demands and got into the passenger seat.

The woman set the navigation to the setting for home when Killa pulled from the parking lot. She then leaned over and pulled him from his pants. A ride up the scenic Pacific Coast Highway is a delight in itself but getting some head at the same damn time is the shit!

Get mad all you like but white girls give the best head. Killa had trouble driving with half his dick in her head. The huge diamond on her hand that stroked the portion of his dick not in her mouth explained why she was wanted dead. When her tonsils tickled his head, he exploded. The woman gulped loudly as she swallowed.

"There! That should take the edge off. I intend to be fucked. I don't want to make love or merely have sex. I want you to fuck the dog shit out of me." She demanded. "Lord knows my husband can't do it. he lacks both the equipment and stamina. Makes billion dollar movies but...."

Killa held his tongue at the ungrateful tirade. In fact, it kind of pissed him off. By the time they reached the huge gated mansion she called home, he had changed his mind about fucking her first. Now he couldn't wait to kill her.

"7, 9, 5, 3." She recited giving him the code to open the gate. The fact that she still hadn't even asked his name yet, popped in his head again.

The same code in reverse caused the large front door to the stately home to open on its own. Killa fought the urge to say, 'wow!' when they stepped into the grand master foyer. He didn't have time to admire the place because the woman marched up the circular steps. He fell in line behind her, watching her ass jiggle under the short dress.

A set of double doors opened to a bedroom suite larger than the entire apartment Killa grew up in. The woman let the dress fall as Killa pulled out his phone and dialed. She was naked before it even rang once. The sight of her firm body made him want to hang up and call back later.

"Who on earth could you possibly be calling at a time like this?" She demanded with a frown.

"Your husband." He said and put the call on speaker.

"Hey slut, looks like you got yourself in a bit of trouble this time." Her husband laughed in the phone.

"What's the meaning of this Harold? What's going on here? Who are you?" She fussed at both men.

"He's a hired killer you stupid bitch! Looks like you bought the wrong nigger home this time!" The man laughed.

Killa frowned at both his nigger comment and her asking who he was with his cum in her belly. Names are to be exchanged before body fluids. He would have let the slander pass if Harold would have shut the fuck up but he wouldn't, so Killa decided to kill him too. That was before the invitation.

"Yeah Sheryl, you bringing all kinds of niggers and spics into our home. Fucking and sucking them in our bed! My bed; you ungrateful piece of trailer trash. I save you and what have you given me in return except disgrace and dishonor."

"Fuck you Harold! You have some nerve! You don't think I know about what you're up to! Your numerous affairs with secretaries! Actresses! Whores! I know, I know!" She shouted at the phone.

"They were white Sheryl. You fucked niggers. Black, nappy headed, thick lipped, disco dancing, pop locking, corn row wearing, fried chicken eating, loud talking, high fiving, all on Facebook telling all their business niggers! Now a nigger is going to kill you. Good bye Sheryl." Harold ranted and hung up.

Sheryl was fuming. "How much to spare me and kill him instead!" She demanded.

"There's no sparing you." Killa admitted plainly. He couldn't do it even if he wanted. Not with the black mob's threats against his family. He didn't want to anyway because he despised adulterers. Sure he fucked around on Kitty but she wasn't his wife. A covenant with God must be kept.

"Well kill him too then. I'll give you a hundred grand right now. Lord knows I have no use for it." She pleaded.

Killa agreed and she handed over the cash. She accepted her fate and submitted by turning around and kneeling in front of him. They say when in Rome do as the Romans, so since they were in LA, he put her in an official L.A.P.D. choke hold. Sheryl went limp after her air was cut off but Killa squeezed for a full minute. He let her body fall on its side and checked her pulse. She was no longer with us.

****

A trip to L.A would not be complete without some good California chronic and pussy. California has some of the best vagina on the planet. The combination of sun and sea air gives it a taste and texture like nowhere else. Its second only to New York followed closely by Atlanta, Dallas and Detroit too and lets not forget about Johnstown, PA. But let's not lose focus.

The killer felt more like a rock star cruising through Los Angeles in the roof-less coupe. A long line of scantily clad women caught his attention so he glided over to investigate. Every woman on the line to get in the club was at least a high seven or eight which meant the place was full of dime pieces. In other words, it was the place to be. He could have plucked one or two even from the line, hell, he wouldn't have had to come to a complete stop but he decided to grab a drink and chill.

"I shouldn't be long." Killa told the valet, slipping him a C-note along with the keys. His intention was to bag the baddest chic in the club and take her back to his room and gut her. He checked out the best Cali had to offer as he ordered a drink.

"I do believe that is her!" He told himself when he spotted a nice caramel colored beauty on the dance floor. He tossed his drink back and went to investigate.

As he drew near, he saw she had a head full of hair that fell to the middle of her back that swayed with her as she swayed to the music. She had a coke bottle shape like nothing he'd seen before, a perfect hour glass plump mounds of breast squeezed from the top of the dress and her ass was so round: It was unreal. Her long eyelashes batted over her green eyes.

"Excuse us." Killa said politely as he rudely stepped between her and the guy she was dancing with. He lowered his head and slinked away while she fixed her mouth to protest. A quick glance over the assertive man killed any complaints.

Gangstas don't dance but they do boogie so Killa did the same two-step he'd been doing since he was two. Meanwhile, she was doing the new fat-fat dance like a pro. She turned around and pressed her fat ass against his crotch and got an immediate reaction.

"Dayum!" She exclaimed, reaching behind her and grabbing his erection.

"He likes you." Killa smiled. "Let's go somewhere so yall can be formally introduced."

"Let's." She said taking the lead off the dance floor. "My name is Daphine by the way."

"Uh, ke, ki, Killa." Killa said, failing to come up with a good club name. Her real name was Earline but Daphine sounds better in the club.

Dirty talk, gropes and feels on the ride to the hotel had him hard and her wet when they arrived. He parked the borrowed Bentley and rushed her up to the room. Since it was already established that they were there to fuck, Killa stripped as soon as they walked in. Seconds later there was nothing but a smirk.

"Excuse me. Let me use your restroom so I can take off all this stuff, so we can really get to it." Daphine giggled.

"Um....ok?" He replied, wondering why she couldn't strip right there. Watching a woman undress is technically foreplay after all. He shrugged it off and lit a blunt, that's foreplay too. Killa sat back on the bed smoking until a strange woman appeared from the bathroom.

"What the fuck! Who are you?" Killa shouted as he scrambled for his pistol. He couldn't believe he got caught slipping but wasn't going out without a fight.

"You so silly. It's me Daphine." The woman insisted.

Now Killa was really confused and it showed on his face. The voice was the same but nothing else. Instead of the long flowing hair, this chic had none. She was several inches shorter and twenty pounds heavier. The coke bottle shape was now that of a milk jug and the plump breasts were replaced by the lopsided titties facing straight down. Her nice round ass must have run off with the long lashes and green eye. This was Earline.

Killa frowned and rushed gun high into the bathroom. That's where he found Daphine. The sexy dress stood up stiffly on its own still holding its hour glass shape. The long hair looked like a ferret lying on the counter next to the eyes and lashes. He could only laugh at himself. He left the club with Beyonce and ended up with sideshow Bob.

Killa went back into the room and fucked sideshow Bob; twice.

****

Harold pulled into his gated estate that next morning with a Cheshire grin pasted on his face. He had produced a ton of blockbuster movies but today he was about to try his chops at acting. He was about to discover his murdered wife and perform the 911 operator, then news and talk shows. it would be great publicity for his new movie in theaters near you. He made a mental note to give his wife's Bentley to his new secretary as he walked past in the circular driveway. The girl had been playing hard to get but the V-12 should part those thighs.

"My wife! Oh my G.... wait.....ok, Oh my God, my wife!" He practiced as he climbed the stairs up to the master bedroom. it cracked him up practicing his own script. Yeah it was real funny, big laughs until he walked in and saw Killa standing there.

"Who the fuck are you?"

"Me baws? Ise just a no count nappy headed nigga." Killa said in his best black Sambo voice and then broke into a little tap dance for master. "What's the matter baws? We sick?"

"You're the killer?" Harold asked, looking over at his dead wife.

"Nope, you are." Killa replied producing his gun. Come to find out you were so distraught about killing your wife, you decided to check out."

"I.... what?" The movie producer snapped. Instead of explaining Killa demonstrated. He walked over and forced the gun into the man's hand. He put up a good fight as he made it up to his temple. Killa pulled the trigger and let him and the gun fall to the thick carpet: The perfect murder/suicide.

"You guys really do make a nice couple." He chuckled over his shoulder to the corpses as he left.

Jihad had a guy who could make Killa's borrowed Bentley disappear. He drove his friend to the airport, filling him in on his new way of life. The life long friend's exchanged pounds and hugs that served as good byes until they saw each other again.

Chapter 14

The extra hundred grand Killa earned from the side job would help him in his exit plan. Fuck the Black Mob, he wasn't going to keep doing their dirty work. Sure it was fun but fuck them.

Knowing his escape would jeopardize his family, he would have to move them somewhere safe. He used some of his fortune on emergency exits. He thought about pulling a Charlie Sheen and moving both Kitty and Sincerity in with him.

"Nah, them chics would kill each other....or me!" He laughed out loud. He was right too; two alpha females could not co-exist under the same roof. Make that three because grandma was a handful too.

The only real option was murder. The Black Mob had to go. He would have to kill all of them so he could live. He of course had no problem with that. He would just have to be patient and play his position until he could strike. He was cool with that until they pushed the issue.

"Woosa" Killa said, exhaling when his business line rang. It always took a lot out of him to listen to that voice that rung his phone. Assuming it was details of his next job, he quickly opened it to view. What he saw took his breath away. There was Sincerity and his newborn son. She was smiling and waving to the camera like there was no danger but how, why would the Black Mob have it!

"He is so adorable. I bet he looks just like his father." The nurse from the hospital cooed as she came into the shot.

"They are twins! Sincerity gushed lovingly. The video was shot in her apartment which shook Killa to his very core. It stopped abruptly and the phone rang.

"Hey buddy!" The voice sang in its sarcastic yet sinister tone that Killa despised. "Cute kid."

"Listen to me very, very carefully. I have no idea what you're up to but you just went too far. My child yo? I'm going to kill you. Not just you but everybody you know. Everybody you've every met. I'm goi......"

"Blah, blah, blah. You are so dramatic! Ok, so I sent Yolo to look in on your family. Big deal, you killed an associate of ours!" Why?" The voice demanded.

"What the fuck are you talking about?" Killa shot back, confused. "I kill who you paif me to kill."

"Uh, Harold; the movie producer. Don't think I bought that suicide shit one bit! You did that shit. He had too much shit on the table to check out. Besides he hated that nigger loving bitch of a wife. Had we not benefited from his death that video you just saw would have been a cooking show. You would have watched Yolo dice that bastard baby up and sauté it with onions and scallions. Now stop fucking playing with me! Kill a fly or step on an ant without my permission and I'll kill your whole family. And guess what? You'll still work for me!"

"I'm sorry." Killa said sheepishly. The show of contrition was a good look and it worked. He needed the watching eyes to blink long enough for him to move his people to higher ground. A flood was coming and it was about to get bloody.

"Well, that's better." The voice said so calmly, you could hear the smile over the line. "Get some rest because we have a lot of work coming your way."

"That's what's up." Killa agreed and clicked off. At the same time he was reaching for his satellite phone.

"Hey baby, I was...."

"Move now!" Killa demanded, cutting his grandmother off in mid-sentence.

The phone went dead immediately as Deidra put the well-planned, well-rehearsed plan in motion. A bag was already packed and waiting by the door. She grabbed it on the way out as she called Sincerity. As soon as she got the call, Sincerity grabbed her packed bag and fled the apartment. The women met in the parking lot where their get away vehicle was parked. Cars were changed in Manhattan, then again in Jersey as they headed to the hideout.

Several hours later, Killa received the call that his family was safe. Kitty too was ducked off at their secluded home which gave him some breathing room. Good thing too, cuz he had some un-authorized killing to do.

****

The Man Boy Love Association was having a jamboree in Denver, Colorado. Men from all walks of life from all over the country were in attendance. There were judges and doctors, priest and pastors, police and firemen, teachers and bus drivers and of course little league coaches. Oh, and one killer or Killa to be precise, one murderously dangerous man on a mission.

The club rented a mountain lodge to accommodate the large turn-out of over one hundred pedophiles. Vacations were taken and excuses made to leave wives and families behind. This was a grand affair; a who's who of booty bandits.

Day one was the scheduled meet and greet, where the sick men could catch up and new members introduced. A grand catered dinner of surf and turf followed by movie night. On display would be the latest in child porn. Day two, there would be an auction where young boys, new and used would be bought, sold and traded. Killa planned to cancel day two.

"Looks heavy, need a hand?" a thirty something rather normal looking black man asked as Killa lifted his suitcase out of the trunk of his rental car.

"Um, sure." Killa replied, amused by the irony. Dude was going to carry in the explosives that were going to level the lodge, killing him and everyone else inside.

Killa looked oddly at the clean-cut man. He looked so normal, even wore a wedding band. Of the hundred or so men, less than five percent were black men. Not that black men don't molest kids, they just don't join clubs about it. He wondered if dude wasn't in the wrong place, maybe he got his dates mixed up. Then he spoke.

"Man, I've been waiting on this for months! I was so excited last night; I was hard as a rock! My wife thought it was for her and climbed on top of it. Oh, I hated being inside of her." He groaned, like he wanted to spit. "I swear, I get more turned on by my sons than her."

"Do you have insurance? Will they be taken care of if you get blown up or say, shot in your head?" Killa asked, entertaining the thought of whipping his pistol out and murdering him on the spot.

"Do I! That's what I do, sell insurance!" He beamed proudly. The whole way up to Killa's room, he went on and on about different plans, as if he wanted to sell him a policy. Killa really wanted to kill him then.

Once they made it up to the room, Killa thanked and dismissed the man. He smiled knowing his family would soon be both rid of him and well taken care of.

The meet and greet was in full effect when Killa slipped out and up to his room. He made several trips back and forth as he rigged the theater with explosives. Soon the large room was laced with two hundred pounds of high explosives. He intended to stay away long enough to miss his own introduction, since non-members were expected to take the podium. No such luck, his name was called the second he returned. Not wanting to blow his cover before he could blow them up, he took the stage.

"Um...Hello." He said tentatively into the mic, causing the room to explode into cheers. "My name is Xavier and I um...I'm a man who loves boys." Killa got out almost choking on the mantra. Again the room exploded in cheers and claps. These dudes really liked boys. Killa went on stammering and stuttering bits and pieces of what he gleamed from previous speeches, until he got down.

Child molesters or no child molesters, the man boy love dudes knew how to put on a dinner. The thick steaks melted like butter and the huge lobster tails were cooked to perfection. The salad was garden fresh crisp and the best wines to wash it all down. Likewise, the dessert menu offered more delightful dishes.

"And now for tonight's entertainment!" The host, a Midwest middle age college professor announced.

Killa wanted to make his escape during the movement but got caught up in the stampede. Good thing the explosives weren't on a timer because he was momentarily trapped. The bombs were set off by a cell phone that was safely in his rental. He ended up in the middle of the theater surrounded by pedophiles. This is where things went from bad to worse.

It was bad when the huge screen filled with the most disgusting images he had ever seen. Mind you this is the same man who blew up a packed funeral home; the same man who hacked men and women into bite size pieces with a hot machete. But that shit on that screen!

It got worse when he turned his head to escape the view only to see the men feverishly pulling on their penises. If he had the detonator, he might have set it off then and put himself out of this misery.

"Excuse me. Pardon me." Killa said, making his way through the masturbating men. He rushed from the theater and towards his rental car.

"Hold up." The insurance salesman called out, rushing to catch up.

"Shit!" Killa fumed at the interruption. "Come on, get in." The men jumped into the car and Killa drove a safe distance away and parked. He got out with the cell phone and so did his guest. He dialed the number, pressed send and smiled at the results.

"Oh my God! What just happened?" The insurance agent screamed.

"I blew the building up." Killa said proudly.

"Blew it up? Are you crazy! You just killed one hundred fifteen people!"

"Make it an even one sixteen." Killa said pulling his gun. The man turned to run but only made it two steps before being gunned down. "Well, that was fun!"

Chapter 15

Harris County, Texas is a large, sprawling mass of land containing the large sprawling city of Houston. There he would be able to blend in and live life; would have, if not for his thirst. The doctor was no vampire but did have a blood lust.

Doc fought off his demons as best he could. He confined himself in his apartment for as long as they would allow. After a month of movies and masturbation, he ventured out into the night. Nothing serious, a cold beer or two. Maybe some good, hot Spanish pussy and perhaps murder. Maybe, maybe not.

"Hola mamacita." Doc said in his second language he perfected during his time away.

"Sup. The average looking Latina replied. She was born and raised here and spoke very little Spanish herself.

Doc had chosen the small, local bar to avoid crowds and cameras. He chose her because she had a pretty smile and long neck.

"Can we go somewhere and talk?" He asked attempting to bride her with his best smile.

"You mean go some where and fuck don't you?" She corrected with a knowing smile. She was with it if he was willing to part with a little cash. The woman wasn't a prostitute but would fuck for money. Yes, there is a difference.

"Well, um yes we could fuck. Fucking is good!" Doc noddd in agreement. He stood and extended his hand to lead her away as he paid the tab.

"Can I borrow thirty bucks?" She asked, trying to count how much money he had.

"Sure" He agreed quickly, peeling a ten and twenty from the rest. As soon as it touched her palm, she took off across the room.

Doc twisted his lips, watching her rush across the bar to a booth containing a couple of young Latino men. He would have assumed one was her pimp when she handed the money over to him. His giving her something in return confirmed it was a drug transaction. Users make the best victims, disposable.

"Ready!" She announced practically bouncing when she returned. She placed her arm in the crook of his and off they went.

Doc's small apartment was a short walk away, so they made the short walk. Small talk filled the void and they soon arrived. He unlocked the door and stepped aside so she could enter.

"After I hit this shit. I'ma fuck your brains out!" She cheered as she produced a small tin package. Doc watched curiously as she dumped the chunky brown powder onto his coffee table. She made four small lines and snorted them, alternating nostrils until they were depleted.

True to her words, she felt the effects immediately and attacked. She stripped in one second and had him in her mouth a second later. After sucking him fully erect, she mounted him backwards and rode him towards Mexico. Doc didn't quite make it to the border and came with a grunt.

"Let's go take a shower." He suggested, still gasping for air. He liked using the shower to cut women up, made clean up easier.

"Nah, I'm cool." the nasty little woman said, jumping off his penis and into her panties in a single bound.

"How's about another thirty bucks?" He said, reversing the process. She peeled the pissy panties off and followed him into his room; followed him to her death.

As soon as they entered the room, Doc slipped his belt around her neck and pulled. The will to live combined with the dose of heroine gave the girl more fight than he bargained for. The small woman thrashed, kicked and clawed for dear life as the doctor held on for dear death. Slowly, she wore down and collapsed with him on her back.

"When!" Doc gasped out of breath when he finally squeezed all the life out of her.

He was rock hard from the struggle and she was naked so. Doc shrugged and pushed inside of her again. He fucked the body until he bust another quick nut. As soon as he pulled out, out came the tools.

Doc broke the body down and bagged the parts. Later that night, he drove around town distributing the parts in various dumpsters. Later that morning those parts began turning up. By that afternoon, the Black Mob got the news.

****

"Is that the fuckin guy! Tell me this is not the fuckin guy! That's the fuckin guy!" Casper shouted in his classic Brooklyn accent.

The Baron looked at him, then the man on the screen, then back to Casper. He didn't know if that was the fuckin guy and didn't care. Of course he didn't say anything. He never said anything.

The man in the ATM photo was supposed to be a dead man. Good money was paid for his murder so how the fuck was he withdrawing money in Texas! Even the Baron knew this meant trouble.

"Yolo!" Casper screamed, sending his shrill voice reverberating throughout the mansion. "This nigger thinks it's a game! I'll show him!"

Yolo was in the shower aiming the hand-held shower head at her throbbing box. She was on the verge of climax when she heard her name being called. The tone of his voice pushed her over the edge. She loved that tone. It meant somebody had to die.

"Yes boss?" She asked arriving naked and wet into the den.

"I want you to go into the city and murder that old lady! Kill his girlfriend and that bastard baby! Make it ugly. I want a slaughter!" Casper whined. "But put some clothes on first!"

Yolo floored the pedal in the SUV as she raced from Long Island into the city. She was dressed to kill in a killer mini skirt and high heels. Her thong was soaked from anticipating killing the old lady. It reminded her of killing her own grandmother some years back. Someone needs to write a book about this chick one day. YOLO, hmm?

Nightfall had just fallen over the university projects as Yolo pulled in. Most residents were safely tucked away in their units, leaving the courtyard relatively empty. The only ones out were the dealers, the junkies and a group of men smoking a blunt.

She checked her gun and extra clips in her designer purse and got out. The tiny dress showed off her luscious legs and the heels tilted her forward making it look like she had more ass than she really did. All eyes were on her, as she clicked her heels on the concrete.

"A-yo, Queen! Ova here mother earth!" One of the blunt smokers yelled as she walked through the courtyard. The strange greeting caught her attention so she detoured to investigate.

"Did you call me Mother Earth?" Yolo asked, tilting her head to punctuate the question. "Why?"

"Word life. See the black man is God and the black woman is earth." He explained. "Shit you need to let a nigga plant a seed in you so we can produce more Kings and Queens."

"You mean have sex with me?"

"Hell yeah." He cheered to the delight of his goofy friends. They thought they were gods too and enjoyed a good laugh.

"What about you guys, Yall wanna fuck me too?" Yolo asked, turning to the rest.

"Hells yeah!" they cheered together.

"Ok, lemme visit my people and I'll come to your apartment so we can get down with the get down."

"I, uh, see, I stay with my Moms." The first one said, disproving his divinity. If he were really God, he would at least have his own place. The Creator of the heavens and Earth and all in between would at least have his own crib wouldn't he?

"Yeah I'm with my grandma....I can't have no company..." Came two more replies.

"Yo we can go up to the roof! I'll get a blanket." The last one announced. It was a good idea since he lived with his baby momma who wouldn't let him and his friends run a train in the house.

"Okay, go on up to the roof and I'll meet you guys in a few." She said, taking the smoldering blunt from between his lips. She took a hearty pull and passed it back. The young woman had no intentions on having sex with them or any one else for that matter. She was a sick, demented killer but she was no slut. Yolo was saving her virginity for marriage. She had killed to keep it, so giving it away to a group of strange men was comical. Not going to happen. Sending them up to the roof was keeping them from harms way because she was on a murder mission.

Yolo's first stop was to Killa's grandmother. The thought of killing the woman spread a pretty smile on her pretty face. Murder always made her happy. Once inside the building, she pulled a pistol from her purse and screwed on the long silencer on its tips. She concealed the gun behind her back and concealed her malice behind a smile and rang the doorbell.

When no one answered, she ran again and again and yet again. She was startled when a neighbor opened the door and stuck her head out. Her nosey ass heard the bell and wanted to investigate. She had been warned that being nosey was going to get her killed one day. Today was that day.

"Who you looking for?" Mrs Bulgar demanded like if it were her right to know.

"Have you see Mrs. Forrest?" Yolo asked, turning so the gun was out of sight.

"Not in days. She tore outta here with a bag and ain't been seen since. I been watching, she ain't been back."

"Fuck!" Yolo spat and spit a round into her forehead.

She marched over to Sincerity's apartment to kill her and cook the baby. Unfortunately for her, they too were gone by the time she arrived.

Yolo was so hurt at not getting to kill them; she was in tears when she emerged from the building. She walked dejected towards the parking until she remembered her date. It wouldn't be a total loss after all.

"You guys ready for me?" Yolo asked as she walked out onto the rooftop.

"Hell yeah!" Came the orchestrated response. The one with the blanket hurriedly laid it out, being the gentlemen that he was. Yolo, being the lady that she was, shot him in his temple.

Death, well sudden violent murder brings out different reactions in different people. The main one who invited death into their lives by calling Yolo over in the first place took off running. Fear clouded his vision and off the building he ran. Another released his inner bitch and screamed like one. Yolo took aim at his tonsils and fired a shot that cut the sound like a mute button. The sole survivor peed and cried when she turned to him.

"Please don't kill me, please." he begged. Begged so sincerely, he got a pass.

"You wanna live?" She asked aiming the pistol at his face.

"Yes, I wanna live!" He laughed with tears streaming down his face.

"Ok" Yolo shrugged and dropped the gun to her side.

"Walk me to my car. Projects can be dangerous."

"Um. o, o, ok." He stammered and led the way, wiping his tears away like a big boy.

Yolo followed him into the building and down the steps. They exited the building and walked to the parking lot. Everything was fine. He could have lived; would have lived had he not opened his big mouth. A glance over at the cute girl and he had to try her.

"So can we link up? Shoot me your number." He asked and got shot.

"718-555-8923." She recited to his shocked corpse.

That same number appeared on Casper's phone a minute later as she called in to report her progress. She took a deep breath and sighed, preparing to report the first failure of her tenure as in-house murderer.

"Tell me they're all dead!" Casper demanded greedily. He was furious at being disobeyed. It would take blood and lots of it to calm him down.

"No boss. They were gone. According to a helpful neighbor, they got in the wind a few days ago." Yolo whispered sadly.

"Ok, hurry back. You're going to Atlanta!"

Chapter 16

"Ooh baby, I'm finna cum!" Kitty moaned as the climatic currents of electricity tingled in her toes. "It's so wet daddy."

"Let me hear it." Killa demanded. She complied, putting the phone between her legs as she played in her puddle. The squishing sound made his erection throb.

"I can't hold it no more!" She yelled and let go. Kitty screamed, thrashed and kicked from the self-induced nut.

The couple had the best phone sex even if it were one sided. Whenever Killa was off killing he made sure to call in and help her get off. Not that she needed the help but his deep voice in her ear as she masturbated sure didn't hurt. It always made him rock hard but he never participated.

"Mmm, when you coming home daddy?" Kitty purred making him wish he were there now. He really wanted to decline the sudden, urgent job. Something felt off about this one, ominous even.

"Tomorrow" He replied, as his target stepped from his house. He was sent to Richmond, VA to murder a mid-level dealer. What was strange was that the hit came without any of the usual theatrics. No instructions or special request, jus a picture text saying, 'kill him.'

"That's perfect! I have a surprise for you!" She sang.

"O baby, you know I hate surprises." Killa said, seriously. Who could blame him since he was technically on the run for multiple murders and facing the death penalty in several states. Yeah he could do without surprises.

"Fine then, spoiled sport." Kitty pouted, causing her man to smile visualizing her pretty bottom lip poked out. "My momma is coming to town! I can't wait for her to meet you."

"A-yo don't bring her to the house! Put her in a hotel." He blurted, sounding far more harsh than intended.

"It's like that? You don't wanna meet my momma? You make me sick!" Kitty cried and hung up.

"Love you too." Killa laughed into the deadline. He called back to explain but got the voicemail. He certainly wasn't going to leave a message. He called again and again, got a voicemail. Again, he hung up and decided he would wait until he got home to straighten it.

"Make me damn sick!" Kitty told his name on her phone screen. She climbed out of bed on wobbly legs from the orgasm and hit the shower. Her mother would be landing soon so she had to get to the airport. "And she aint staying in no damn hotel!"

Killa followed the dealer with mixed emotions. The hit was too easy, why? He kept wondering. Dude was an average guy who drove an average car and more average clothes. He had no security so why send in the big guys. Hell you could have broke his woman off to murder him. He had no clue the man was a sacrificial lamb: A decoy.

"Oh well." Killa shrugged and made his move. The target stopped at the red light on Bond Street and Killa whipped around from behind and pulled along side of him. The sudden move caused the man to turn to investigate just like Killa knew he would. When he turned his face towards him, he pumped two quick shots at his nostrils. Easy, too easy.

****

"So, when can I meet this mystery man of yours?" Kitty's mom asked dubiously.

"Tomorrow. He's away on business and I see that look on your face!"

"What?" Her mother giggled, playing innocent.

"Mmm hmm, there really is a boyfriend momma....this time." She insisted. She had made up men before to make up for being so picky and not having one. "Matter fact, we'll see him first thing in the morning right here cuz I gotta pick him up when his flight lands."

Kitty kept her word about not bringing her mother to the house but wasn't putting her in any hotel either. Since they dined downtown, she decided they would go to the rarely used condo. They only stopped here for sex and Kitty loved it. He really put on when they did it in the condo. Men do that when they know they are being watched.

"Wow, this is nice!" Kitty's mom gushed as they entered the plush high-rise building.

"I know. I just hate that we....." She replied, cutting herself off from giving too much info.

She helped her diva of a mom with way more baggage than needed for the short stay. Kitty unconsciously darted her eyes around as she noticed her man does every time they came. When she was convinced there was no threat, she produced the keys and unlocked the door. She stepped aside so her mother could enter and found the threat inside.

"Well, hello." Kitty's mom said with a smile to the young lady sitting on the sofa.

"Who the hell are you!" Kitty demanded, coming in behind her instead of turning around and running for her life, which, well would have been better, much better.

"My name is irrelevant!" Well that's not my name, but knowing my name is irrelevant cuz....anyway, just call me Yolo."

"Ok, so Yolo, what the fuck are you doing in my man's condo?" She demanded hotly, assuming Killa had been keeping some chic in the unit. She was ready to put her hands on her and toss her out on her blonde fro.

"You think? Oh no! Un uh, you got it all wrong." Yolo laughed.

"So who are you and why are you here?" Kitty said, moving on her. Momma too kicked her shoes off to help. Wouldn't be the first time momma and daughter whooped some ass.

Only Yolo didn't do ass whooping. She pulled out a gun. Then she pulled out a huge knife. Then she pulled some real bullshit.

****

"Wow, really?" Killa chuckled aloud as Kitty's phone went straight to voicemail again. He had been calling all morning before boarding his flight and now again that he touched down in the A.

Even though Killa had the IQ of a rocket scientist, it didn't take one to figure out that she wasn't coming to pick him up. Kitty could hold world class grudges when she wanted to. She had no problem going days without speaking to him when angry. She would still fuck him though. Reason being, why deprive herself of some good wood just because he screwed up. No sense denying herself of a nut just because he acted like one. Yeah, women could learn a lesson from Kitty.

"A-yo, I'm going to the house to shower and change. Let me know what hotel you're at so I can take you and momma to brunch. And um....you nawmean? I'm saying though, you know what I'm saying....I..shit!" Killa stammered until the recording time elaspsed. He manned up and called right back to get it out. "I love you. There! I said it, hope you're happy."

Killa strolled through the airport exchanging smiles with passersby as he passed by. He arrived at the public train and bought a ticket. a few stops later, he got off and found one of his many vehicles stashed around the city. The universal key he had fitted to all his cars opened it remotely as he neared. It cost a pretty penny but it beat walking around with a big ass ring full of keys like a janitor.

Thoughts of both Kitty's smile and thick thighs filled the long ride to the house. Those same thoughts kept him in the hotel in Richmond instead of sampling some of Virgina's VJ.

Back at the house, he washed all traces of travel under the shower. With making a good first impression his goal, Killa selected a pair of slacks and shirt from the 'his' said of the 'his and hers' closet. Italian loafers completed the casual outfit. A check of his phone showed Kitty finally hit back, only the stark message had put him on alert.

'At the condo' was all the text said, causing him to frown. She had been excavating his soul for his feelings and now when he tells her he loves her she replies, 'at the condo.'

He retrieved a fifty caliber desert eagle intended to make a mess of anyone if anything happened to his girl. A bulletproof vest was a last minute addition to his outfit, as he left the house. It didn't quite match but eh...

The ride into the city was pure torture. He wanted to put the pedal to the metal and rush but that would not be a good look with a car full of weapons. A police stop now would make history. Instead, Killa paced himself with the other cars and held his breath.

"Our boy is here." Yolo announced into her bluetooth when she saw Killa pull up. She was watching through a high powered scope attached to a high powered rifle. One squeeze on the trigger could end this story now. "Let me finish it, please!"

"No! Not yet!" Casper screamed on the verge of one of his hissy fits. "He has to make penance first."

"Oh, ok!" Yolo pouted, showing her age and releasing the death grip on the trigger. "So what now?"

"Nothing. Trust me; our boy will come looking for us. He won't find us but then you can kill him."

"My pleasure." Yolo smiled at both the sight of the handsome murderer and the thought of murdering him. 'He could get it thought.' She mused to herself as he disappeared into the building.

"All that noise! I knew 'you people' would be trouble when you moved in!" The elderly neighbor chided when she saw Killa emerge from the elevator. She berating him with her racist remarks while her lap dog yapped like it was her hype man. It was her Flava Flav barking, 'yeah boyee'.

Killa ignored her, just like he did every time he came to the condo. It never failed. Anytime he visited, she was there waiting. When he rushed into the unit, time stopped along with his heart. If he didn't already know, he would have sworn someone had painted the condo red. Only he knew the smell of blood all too well. He had been frozen in place for so long that he ran out of breath and had to tell himself to take another. He took a deep breath and stepped fully into the unit. Luckily the threat was no longer present because his large gun fell from his numb hand.

"No." He moaned softly at the sight of his Kitty. The lone tear then ran down his face wasn't sorrow. It was rage. The man who killed for fun, killed for practice and killed for pay was now mad. The already red room became even redder from the fury.

He would have expected nice clean bullets to the head. That's murder. But these women were mutilated by a very sick individual. Yolo had hacked the mother and daughter to pieces then put them back together mismatched. The macabre jigsaw puzzle made his stomach bubble. The killer also played in the blood, drawing juvenile pictures on the wall. Killa wasn't sure how long he had been stuck but his business phone restarted time.

"Your fault, you know." Casper teased childishly when Killa answered the line. "Told you to stop playing with me."

"You did" Killa replied softly. "You know I'm coming for you don't you? I will find you."

"Ooh, I'm so scared! Whatever. Look, tell you what. Go finish your job and I'll wait until after you're dead to kill the rest of your family. If not, I'll feed them to you. Yolo cooks a baby like nobody's business." Casper hung up and sent the file.

"Huh?" Killa asked at the surveillance pictures of Doc. The first was of him removing cash from an ATM machine. This was obviously how they found and tracked him. The notion sparked an idea in Killa's mind as well. That is how he could locate the voice and silence it forever.

He watched footage of Doc leaving a run down bar with a run down woman. Next was new footage of that same woman being found all over town. Five dismembered women in a short span of time. The documentary jumped from the mainland down to Costa Rica. Some-one had done their homework and linked him to the grisly murders there as well. It showed the distraught Chief of Police, holding the jar containing his daughter's head. Killa looked into the man's eyes and felt him. It was the exact same feeling he felt in his heart. The video ended at Doc's front door. It panned out, giving the exact address.

Killa could not and would not leave his woman like that. Thought of strangers collecting her and putting her in a bag didn't sit well with him. Since she would have to be cremated, he decided to do it himself. He went down to the car to retrieve the metal five gallon gas can. The bitter old bitty next door hurled obscenities and 'you peoples' as he came and went. He just smiled knowing she was about to be cremated too. He placed the gas can on an eye of the electric stove and turned it on.

"I'm coming for you." Killa voiced, turning around in a circle to speak to the unseen cameras and mics.

Left led to the elevator and out while right took him to the nosey neighbor's house. Killa turned right and used his should to unlock and open her door. She opened her big mouth to scream but the big gun wouldn't allow it.

"Nig..." Was all she got out before the huge triangular barrel was slammed into her mouth. It forced her top dentures down her throat.

Killa snarled just like the lap dog nipping at his heels as he lifted her off the floor by her frail neck.

"Call me nigga now!" Killa dared. The gun was too far down her throat for speech so the feisty old bag called him niggers with her eyes. He pushed the gun further until it touched her spine and fired.

The fifty caliber slug took the back of her skull completely off. It and her wig fell to the ground right before her brain fell out of the hole. That shut the little mutt up.

The sound of the gas can exploding told him it was time to leave. It was time to kill.

Chapter 17

When Killa left the flaming condo building, he was a man on a mission. He drove the car to the train, and then switched to a bus to be sure he wasn't followed.

He ended up in the Eastwyck apartment complex in the Atlanta suburb of Decatur. This is where his cousin, the original Dope Boy, Cameron Forrest once lived. This is where his emergency car was parked. It contained everything needed to go on the lamb, including cash, fake ID, clothes and of course guns.

Killa pulled out of the complex and jumped on Highway I-20 headed west. His destination was Louisville, Kentucky but he was not going for the Derby. No this was where the bank that made his deposits was located. Being in a new city afforded him anonymity, here he was invisible.

This city, like most cities had a black population and a hood. Its hood like most hoods was full of sex, violence and drugs. That of course was right up his alley because Killa like pussy, murder and blunts. An episode of his favorite show, 'The First 48' was shot here once a week it seemed. Its new executive producer was now in town. An extended stay motel would be his home base for his homework.

The First National Bank of Kentucky was a funding source of the compensation for his corporate killings. This was where he would start. Now he had to figure a way in. He could run up in there on some Wild West type shit, jump on the counter and make them tell him what he wanted to now about the sender. That was the old Killa, the less refined Killa. The new Killa was going to fuck one of the pretty tellers and let her tell him what he wanted to know.

Now all he had to do was pick one, not just any one but the right one. There were several for him to choose from in an assortment of sizes, shapes and colors. A jet black, six-footer caught his eye as did a short chubby light skin girl. The lone ratchet girl with pounds of weave stacked high on her head might do as would the flirtatious white girl. He had all but settled on a pretty brown thing until she walked by.

The cute petite woman caught Killa's eye as she walked by. She was the type of chic some superficial dude might not look at since she rocked none of the superficial embellishments superficial women wore. Her tasteful business suite fell just above her knee and was modestly fitted to her small shapely frame. Five two, a buck twenty five-ish with no fake lashes or contacts. The shoulder length hair that seductively veiled one eye was mostly hers but he couldn't tell. And that smile!

Killa didn't even realize he had stepped out of line and followed her until he found himself at her desk staring down at her. The name plate on the desk read C. Sampson, Loan Advisor and he pondered on what the C stood for.

"Can I help you?" Ms. Sampson asked, snapping him into the present.

"You most certainly can." He said quickly and took the seat facing her. "May name is Orenthal James." He said gazing through her eyes and into her soul.

"And how can I assist you Mr. James?" She said, feeling a current of electricity surge through her.

"My company is expanding here and we need to secure a small loan to cover operating expenses." He said smoothly.

"Oh, we can definitely help you with that!" She said, flashing that smile ate him.

"Great." Killa replied and began filling out the paperwork. The dummy company he had set up had checked out and the loan was quickly approved.

"We can cut a check in a day or two." Ms. Sampson said, signing the paperwork. She then slid it across the desk for him to do the same.

"Chrishawn!" He cheered at seeing what the C stood for. He would have never guessed that. In his mind he'd settled on Chrissy.

"Huh?" She laughed curiously at the outburst.

"Oh, I had been wondering what the C stood for." He admitted. "Can I call you Chrishawn?"

"Um, sure everyone calls me by my first name." She agreed.

"No, I meant can I call you, Chrishawn; on the phone, personal not business?" He offered diving back into her eyes.

Another one of those killer smiles accompanied the head nod that came with her cell number. He called that night and they spoke until that morning. That next night, they starred across a small table in a small Indian restaurant.

"Would you think less of me if I slept with you so soon?" Killa asked seriously. He was seriously asking if he could hit.

"General yes, but I guess I'll give you a pass." She said, answering both questions. "Check please!"

After paying the tab, they rushed back to her apartment and stripped.

"Wow!" Killa exclaimed at the sigh of Chrishawn in the matching black and pink bra and panty set.

"Wow is right." She said equally impressed with his body.

Killa was never big on kissing, until tonight. An hour passed kissing, sucking and tasting mouths, lips and tongues. They groped each other while they kissed and when his finger slid inside of her foreplay time was over.

"Roll over on your stomach." Killa ordered with a mischievous grin. Chrishawn smiled back and complied.

He began with her Achilles heel, giving it a nibble. He planted soft kisses up her calf and licked the back of her knees. Thighs are for sucking so he sucked hers. He then smiled at the small round ass before biting it. The heat from between her legs warned his cheek as he did; reminding him of the hot box they use to deliver pizza. He avoided the tattoo the small of her back because dudes love to skeet on tattoos, especially of other dudes' names. He admired it and another tattoo of designs and stars further up her back.

Using one hand, he guided himself to the entrance of the vagina that would be his for the night. A warm, safe home for the evening. He pushed the hair away from her neck and latched on with his teeth. Killa growled as he pushed inside of her. He learned this position from watching animal planet. This was how lions fuck.

"Mmm" Chrishawn moaned as he sank deeper inside of her. She arched her back, tilting her ass to allow him all the way inside. She even gave up the small crevice she had been saving for someone special. Right about now, Killa was feeling special.

Killa wanted to pull out so he could get a nice stroke going but the thought of pulling out just didn't sit well with him. Instead, he rested against her cervix and grinded in clockwise motion. The move earned another moan and she got in on the act by rotating her hips counter clockwise.

They growled, moaned and rotated until neither could take it any more. Chrishawn was first to explode and screamed as she came harder than anytime in her life, causing a puddle to form under her. Killa contemplated busting a nut inside of her. Fuck it, if she got pregnant, he would just marry her and live happily ever after. But, he knew there would be no happily ever after for him. He was destined to die as violently as he lived. At the last second he pulled out and shot for the stars.

An orgasm is the world's best sedative and Chrishawn was asleep in seconds. She may be a pretty little petite thing but she snored like a biker. As soon as her snores filled th room, he got up and got to work. He installed a password program that made quick work of the system's security. The password turned out to be the tagline of her favorite author.

"I got next." He mouthed as he entered the code. No wonder she made it into one of his books.

After copying files, Killa erased his program and his tracks from her laptop. He slipped the twenty five thousand dollars from the bank loan into her purse and prepared to smash out. Would have been gone if he hadn't looked over at the lovely lady on the bed. He slid back in next to her and kissed her awake. "Round two?"

"As long as I get to be on top." Chrishawn agreed. she didn't wait for a reply, just climbed on board. She rode him hard and fast with the ferocity and finality of a soldier going off to war. Another orgasm wracked her and she fell off to the side.

"Mmm, I think I love you." She moaned and started her bike back up. She laid her head on his chest and went back to sleep.

Killa didn't reply. Just kissed her pretty face and slid from under her. He had to be careful not to look down as he dressed for fear he would never leave. He planted one final kiss on the back of her head and slipped off.

Chapter 18

"Hey handsome." Quiana smiled, taking a seat next to the white man at the bar.

"Um, yeah, hey." Doc replied uninterested. The way the drop-dead gorgeous woman was dressed spelled prostitute. He dismissed the pretty smile with the pretty gap and turned back to his drink. He preferred Latin women and their hot boxes.

"Awww, don't be like that." She pouted at the snub. She really didn't care because he wasn't her type either. This was just a job.

"I'm sorry." Doc said sincerely hearing her tone. "I didn't mean to be rude." He ran his eyes over her thick body and couldn't help but wonder if she tasted anything like her brown sugar complexion. His next question was proof that curiosity kills the cat. "You wanna go somewhere and um, talk?"

"Sure!" She said eagerly knowing the um meant fuck "I have a house out in the country."

Doc was so excited about trying out some dark meat; he leaped from the bar without even paying. He made it two feet before getting an earful from the stud tending the bar. The change from the twenty he allowed her to keep soothed her and off they went. Quiana's ass shifted from side-to side as Doc watched in awe. Ma was putting on a great show, but then again she was a professional.

"So how much is this going to cost me?" Doc asked curiously, not that he planned to pay her, and besides what could she buy with her head chopped off anyway.

"You? Not a penny." She said sweetly with a smile and pat on his leg. They made banal small talk as she drove outside of the city limits; way out where nobody could hear you scream.

The GPS unit gave audible directions that she followed. That was proof that erections and common sense are not present to a man at the same time. He never wondered why she needed directions to her own home.

"Here we are." Quiana announced, pulling into the driveway of the secluded house.

Doc jumped out and followed her in. He could not resist grabbing a handful of the handfuls of ass on the pretty woman. Her reaction at being groped too should have been a warning.

"Don't touch me!" She barked, slapping his hand away. What prostitute does that? He still followed her into the house like a lamb to slaughter.

"In here." Quiana ordered, leading Doc into one of the bedrooms. He was so thirsty; he hadn't even noticed her ghetto accent was gone. She now sounded like a white girl. Her job was done. "Back in a sec."

"Don't make me wait too long." Doc said, batting his eye in an attempt to be sexy and failing.

"Thank you." Quiana said sweetly as she accepted a stack of cash from the client. She wanted to flirt a little with the handsome man but the look in his eyes prevented.

Now, this is the part where it would be cool if this were a picture book because the look on Doc's face when Killa walked in is beyond words. Killa had a pretty shocked look on his face as well finding the man jumping up and down on the bed butt naked.

"Killa?" Doc shouted in mid-air. He bent his knees when he landed, coming to a complete stop. "What are you doing here?"

"Me! Nigga what are you doing here?" Killa shot back, turning a murderous shade of red. "They slaughtered my woman and went after my family!"

"I had some um...I had a few problems in Central America." Doc stammered, climbing down from the bed.

"Problems? Dude, you was down there cutting bitches heads off. You make it sound like your visa expired or you got a rash! What the hell got into you?" Killa demanded. He knew full well what turned him into a killer. It was his home life, his projects, rap music but what happened to Doc?

"What got in to me?" Doc questioned hotly, walking up on Killa. "What got into me? You! That's what, you. You made it sound so sexy to kill. And you know what? It is! I love that shit and I'm not stopping."

"You are obviously not getting the point of my presence. Why I hired the actress to lure you out here away from the watching eyes of the Black Mob. Why you're in this secluded house, way out here in the country."

"What to kill me? Plu-eeze!" Doc laughed. "Killa, you can't kill me, you can't we're friends. Hell, I'm the only friend you got and I saved your life! You saved my life, we're friends."

Killa could not argue with that reason so he didn't try. The man was right he did save his life. They were friends; no one on earth knew or understood the other like they did.

"Nah, I can't kill you. I'm not going to." Killa sighed. "But, I'm not saving you either."

Doc wanted to say something when his friend turned to leave. Part of him wanted to get dressed and go with him. They could be a team, the deadly duo. Doc and Killa or Killa and Doc. Maybe someone would write a book about them or a movie.

Out in the hallway, Killa nodded a long conversation to the third killer in the house, as they passed each other. It was only a head nod but spoke volumes. The smile on the man's face did not match the ferocity in his eyes. He clutched his large bag tightly and walked into the room.

"Who are you?" Doc demanded to the stranger. The man sat his bad down to remove its contents as he began to speak.

"I am Chief of Police of San Jose, Costa Rica. I believe you know my daughter." He answered, producing the jar containing her head. Again, you should have seen the look on his face.

Chapter 19

It's a long ass ride from Texas to New York but it flashed in the blink of an eye. Killa had murder on his mind the whole trip but still hadn't come up with a plan. Everyone and everything had to die, that much he knew. Pets, plants, guests, it didn't matter, they were dead.

Visions of Kitty's smile kept being interrupted by visions of her mutilated corpse. No, there was no particular plan but it was going to be brutal. When he reached Georgia, he pulled off to see Big Shawn, who specialized in all things brutal.

"The fuck! A-yo son, don't you ever fucking knock?!" Bigs demanded when he found Killa sitting in his living room smoking a blunt at three in the morning.

"Want a pull?" He replied, extending the cigar to him.

"May as well, since its mine!" He quipped, taking the blunt and a seat. "What brings you to town?"

"Yo, I need the same thing you gave my uncle.....the vest." Killa said somberly.

"Yo, why don't I pack a few pieces and come with you?" Bigs suggested. "That was a limited edition. No more of those."

"I don't know what I'm up against. All that matters is that the die. All of them."

Bigs hoisted his large frame from the sofa and headed towards the showroom with Killa in tow. Both men scanned the room for the right weapons of mass destruction.

"This is what you need." Bigs exclaimed, reaching for a sniper's rifle equipped with a large scope and larger silencer. "This baby can shoot the head off a mosquito's dick from a mile away!"

"Yo, do mosquitoes even have dicks?" Killa pondered aloud as he took the weapon. "I'll Google it."

"Take a few of these shits right her. These will clear shit out in a hurry!" The salesman said of a box of grenades.

They collected guns, bullets, bombs and finally a bullet proof vest. Bigs tallied the merchandise and it came to twelve grand.

"I have a coupon." Killa joked as he pulled out a bank roll. He didn't really so instead he peeled off the twelve stacks.

After loading his guns, Killa jumped back onto the highway headed north. He gave the city of Atlanta a long lustful gaze as it passed his window, knowing it could be the last time he saw it. It was that sense of finality that forced him to make one more stop before reaching New York.

Killa navigated the streets of Philadelphia like a native. He pulled to a stop across the street from the North Philly Daycare that was his destination. Destiny put him there just in time because no sooner than he arrived, his son walked out, holding his aunt's hand. Aniya was the same pretty brown color as her late sister and had an identical smile. The proud father got out and followed discretely behind them until they reached the condo Denise once live in. With all the sentimental shit out the way, he was ready to go murder something.

The mansion used as headquarters for the Black Mob was way out in Hampton, Long Island. It was private, secluded and perfect. An eight foot wrought iron fence surrounded the property and beside the three massive Presa-de carnario dogs patrolling the grounds, there was no security. The Black Mob depended more on its reputation and secrecy for protection and since no one could know that Casper really called the shots, there could be no inner circle. But, they did have Yolo.

Yolo sat wide-legged and naked in front of her flat panel computer screen. She was masturbating as usual while surfing the net for porn. Porn actually made her want to kill. Blame that on her childhood but that's another story.

Casper too was engaged in his favorite pass time, getting head. He kept a rotation of strippers in and out for the task. The plush den contained a rarely use stripper pole because the dancers rarely danced. He figured why watch them strip which was only going to make him hard which was going to make him want some head. He cut through the chase to the back of their throats.

Baron did what he did best which was staring off into space. He never spoke, laughed nor smiled. He did enjoy his new digs and plentiful food but not his housemates. Casper was once loyal and grateful but now rude and disrespectful. It was as if he had forgotten who saved his ass, literally, who kept dicks out his mouth and rectum. Oh and that crazy little naked girl, he really didn't like her. She scared him.

Killa did what he did best and lined one of the large dogs in his scope. At the last second, the dog turned in his direction and caught a slug right between his eyes. The way the dog's head exploded made him smile and shoot the next one. It had came over to see what happened to its buddy and got the same. The last one tried to run but didn't get far as Killa brought it down too.

With the security all down, Killa began his approach. The athletic goon scaled the fence in seconds and was on the grounds. He traded his rifle for a pistol and crept forward. Killa ignored the moving truck and rigged the other vehicles with grenades. He attached them to the gas tanks to expound on the explosives.

He slipped into the house through the large doggy doors in the kitchen door. Gun first, Killa crept through the house. In the empty living room he found a candy jar filled with fluffy weed. Knowing the owners wouldn't mind or live to complain, he stuffed a handful into his pocket. He followed his ears upstairs and found his targets.

Both Baron and Casper were receiving blow jobs by strippers. Besides, the food this is what Baron loved next. Almost everyday, Casper had one of the pretty white girls blow him. He was enjoying her head until it exploded.

"Don't move!" Killa demanded to all present, scanning them with his gun.

"I think I should go now." The surviving stripper announced. She came with the other girl but definitely didn't want to go with her.

"I think you should go now too." Killa agreed and sent her with her friend with a silent slug to her forehead.

"Black Mob." Killa chuckled, walking up on the Baron.

"You went after my people? Killed my girl?"

Baron shot a sympathetic glance to Casper for help and got none. Casper stayed mute, content with his bodyguard taking the heat. Baron was mute, not slow and knew he was taking heat for his shit.

"Nothing to say!" Killa demanded and pumped a slug into his knee.

The Baron's mouth opened and a thunderous cry came out. Yolo heard it from her room and jumped up. She quickly donned a vest and grabbed her gun.

"Still nothing?" He asked, sending more shots his way. Casper saw he was busy and eased towards the door. Killa saw him and put a round in his ass. "Get back in here!"

"So sorry." Casper blurted from fear and pain, and let the cat out of the bag. All the air got sucked out of the room at the sound of his voice. This was the smart ass, disrespectful voice that gave the commands; the voice that made the threats.

"You?" Killa asked in confusion, looking back and forth between the two men. "So who is he?"

"That's the Baron. My flunky. The public face of the Black Mob." Casper said suddenly smug.

"Looks like you're gonna need a new face." Killa announced and shot the Baron in his. He didn't know why the unarmed man was so cocky. That's because he didn't see Yolo sneak into the room.

Didn't see her but definitely heard her when her gun discharged. Damn sure felt the slug that slammed into his back. Vest or no vest, getting shot hurts. The impact spun him around and he came up firing. He and Yolo back peddled as they shot each other in their chests. They both fell and popped back up at the same time. They both pulled their triggers and came up empty. Only Killa had an extra clip and Yolo could only watch as he inserted it, as Casper limped out of the room.

"Shoulda shot you in your pretty face." Yolo said with a defiant scowl on her own pretty face. That's when he noticed she was naked beside the vest.

"Well, I'm damn sure gonna shoot you in yours!" He laughed.

"You gonna let Casper just get away?" She offered, hoping for a way out.

"He won't get ar." Killa replied. The sound of an engine starting was closely followed by an explosion. "Not in one piece that is."

"I aint gone beg but I will make you an offer. Ten thousand keys. Straight out of Columbia, spare me and it's yours. Me too; if you want me." Yolo said seductively slinking forward. "Out in that truck!"

"Bitch they aint printed enough money for me to spare you." Killa growled. The attempted bribe and seduction caused him to viciously back hand her to the ground.

"Mmm baby, that turns me on." Yolo moaned up at him. She quickly pulled her vest off and played in her box as Killa watched curiously. "You may as well fuck me first. Don't let me die a virgin."

"A what!" Killa asked and laughed. Chics didn't make it past 15 in his world with their cherries intact. "Get the fuck outta here!"

"It's true! I been saving myself for my husband. I'ma good girl. 'Cept you aint gonna let me live long enough to get a husband." Yolo pouted.

Oddly Killa was slightly turned on at the prospect of a brand new vagina. Those are the best ones. And see, that's how men think, why not fuck a chic if you gonna kill her anyway. He didn't even resist when she crawled over and pulled him out of his pants. Once he grew stiff inside her mouth, Killa shot his knee up and knocked her over.

"You wanna get fucked, I'ma fuck you then!" He growled, grabbing her by an ankle.

Killa shoved himself inside of her roughly causing her to scream from the searing pain. He was shocked at how tight she was until he saw the blood from her ruptured hyman.

"We can be together." Yolo pleaded as he pounded. "We should be together. Imagine our kids!"

Her moans and voice only made him angrier. This was a grudge fuck, consensual rape. It wasn't supposed to feel good. He snatched himself out of her, flipped her over and plunged back inside. Yolo now screamed from pleasure and pain for the pounding.

"Mmm, I'm gonna cum." she whined as the feeling began to build.

The thought of her enjoying the act infuriated him. If he wasn't so close himself, he would have stopped and killed her right then. Again, that's how men think, why not cum in a chick if you're going to kill her anyway. Killa grunted and released just before she did. She began to hum from the orgasm but Killa fired a shot into the back of her dreadlocks. Then another.

"Stupid ass bitch...good pussy though." Killa said, cleaning the semen and blood off himself. A slow smile spread across his face as he scanned the room full of bodies. Nothing is more satisfying than killing your enemies.

"Fuck I'ma do with ten thousand kilo of coke?" He pondered as he drove the cocaine laden truck off the premises.

****

Killa left behind a house full of bodies but not all of them were dead. The hookers were of course deceased with the bullets in their head. The Baron didn't even have a face, so he was gone. Casper was in hundreds of pieces in the yard and Yolo took two to the back of her head...

"Oww." Yolo moaned as her eyes fluttered open. She laid there for several minutes before even trying to move. Slowly, she rolled onto her back wincing from the pain. She reached up and pulled the heavy bullet proof wig off and sighed. Yolo had a concussion, hairline skull fracture and nasty headache but she was alive. Alive and in love.

"Mmm Mr. Killa , I think I love you." She moaned, reaching between her legs again. "But I am so going to kill you!"

The End